FLIGHT *to the* PROMISE

FLIGHT *to the* PROMISE

R. HILARY ADCOCK

WestBow
PRESS
A DIVISION OF THOMAS NELSON

WestBow Press books may be ordered through booksellers or by contacting:

WestBow Press
A Division of Thomas Nelson
1663 Liberty Drive
Bloomington, IN 47403
www.westbowpress.com
1-(866) 928-1240

ISBN: 978-1-4497-1888-6 (sc)
ISBN: 978-1-4497-1889-3 (e)

Library of Congress Control Number: 2011930947

Printed in the United States of America

WestBow Press rev. date: 7/11/2011

DEDICATION

Thanks to my wife and children, who understood and tolerated my time locked away in my home office, the place they call "Dad's Cave."

Thanks to my flight instructors, J. P. and T. K., who became my best friends and whose lives and skills gave me the courage to meet any challenge.

Most of all, thanks to God for the life-changing power of His promises.

"Nation will rise against nation, and kingdom against kingdom. There will be great earthquakes, famines and pestilences in various places, and fearful events and great signs from heaven." Luke 21:10–11

INTRODUCTION

Four American men, each with uniquely different life experiences and each representing one of four stereotypes regarding God, heaven, and matters of the spirit. Unwittingly drawn together by the hand of God, they find themselves on a life-changing journey that celebrates creation, transforms souls, and sets a plan in motion for world events yet to come. In tragedy and joy, through bankruptcy and wealth, and guided by God's Holy Spirit, they are drawn toward a divine and secret plan as the Earth spins closer to the Tribulation.

The heart of the book was inspired by a flight from Phoenix to Las Vegas and the life-changing effects that the experience had on the author. However, the story and the characters are fictional.

CIRCA AD 1985

CHAPTER 1

Young Chester Hamilton Rawlins watched the propeller on the left engine slowly wind down and stop.

The full load of passengers was too much for the right engine. Even with full throttle and the propeller biting hard, they were losing altitude. He needed to find a place to land the crippled airplane and save their lives.

A giant hand rolled the little twin-engine airplane into a steep turn, and the brave young pilot immediately spotted a NASCAR racetrack below. A pileup of racecars were scattered around turn three, but the back straightaway was wide open. It was a tough decision, but sometimes a guy has no other choice.

The hand took over again, banked the crippled airplane into a steep turn, and dove her toward the racetrack straightaway. Then, just when it seemed too late to halt the screaming descent, the nose pulled up, with only a few inches of air between them and disaster.

The landing was hard, and the hand fought to keep the wings level and the nose straight ahead, the tires screeching with each skidding direction change. The airplane slid sideways the last few inches and came to rest next to an overturned red race car with the number 7 emblazoned on the driver's door and a Hot Wheels logo on the undercarriage. The startled racecar drivers all climbed out of their wrecked NASCAR machines and held their helmets in the air, a salute to victory. And in the distance, he could hear the crowded racetrack bleachers explode with cheers, applause, and shouts.

"Chester!"

The sound of Momma's voice invaded the make-believe world of his bedroom floor.

"I see your Daddy's truck comin' up the road!"

Momma always called him Chester.

In less than a second, he was on his feet running toward the door. Hot Wheels racecars and toy airplanes scattered in all directions. As he bolted through the bedroom door, he heard the double blast of the air horns on the roof of Daddy's red Freightliner. He ran through the living room and out the front door where Goldie joined the race. The screen door banged shut in their wake and, as usual, she beat him to the gate.

Chester peered over the four-foot-high white picket fence and watched the west Texas wind clear away the dust stirred up by the big truck and trailer. As the truck rolled to a stop, Goldie assumed her yellow Labrador "heel" position, and her long tail swept the dusty ground near Chester's feet. He hopped up and down with his fists clutched around the fence boards and watched Daddy step down from the cab. Daddy's boots made solid crunching sounds on the gravel roadway as he ambled toward the gate.

Momma walked up behind Chester, wiped her hands on the hem of her kitchen apron, and looked down at her healthy eleven-year-old boy. His copper-red hair reflected the afternoon sun as she combed her fingers through the unruly twirling mass on the back of his head. Chester got Momma's red hair and freckles, and it seemed as though he got Daddy's lanky build. Time would tell.

Avon makeup usually hid Momma's freckles, but that day she had been busy in the kitchen making apple pies for the church potluck. Her hair was twisted up into a bun on top of her head and, without the makeup; her freckles competed with Chester's.

Daddy stepped through the gate, closed it behind him, and cast one last glance at the truck. Then he turned back toward his family. The six-foot-tall trucker pulled a red shop rag out of his back pocket, wiped his hands, and looked down at Chester.

"Look at you boy. I swear Chet you must of grown two inches, and it's only been two weeks."

Daddy always called him Chet.

He scooped Chet up and, unable to hold back any longer, Momma stepped into the hug that she craved, enveloped in the strong arms of her hard-working man. Held there, she breathed in the musk-like scent, mingled with the smell of fresh-cut hay that permeated from his faded blue work shirt. The only other hint of what he hauled that trip were the shards of straw and bits of bailing wire stuck between the planks of the long flatbed trailer.

Goldie ran in circles around the couple as they embraced, with Chet sandwiched between Momma's flour-covered cotton blouse and Daddy's sweat-stained shirt. Entwined as they were, the young family slowly walked into the house together, leaving Goldie on the front porch where she curled up next to the door on her favorite blanket.

Daddy sat on the couch, took off his boots, and then stretched his legs and put his stocking feet up on coffee table. Chet climbed up on the couch next to Daddy. He would like to do the same thing except his legs were not long enough yet. Instead, he took off his shoes, curled his feet under himself sitting Indian style facing Daddy, and suddenly exclaimed, "Daddy, I want to be a pilot when I grow up!"

Seldom caught off guard by the boy's spontaneity, Daddy looked toward the ceiling, appearing to study the globe-shaped light fixture and slowly revolving ceiling fan. Then he put his hands behind his head in a stretching motion and called out, "Baby!" Daddy always called her *baby* when they were at home. "Chet wants to fly airplanes. What do ya think?"

Momma stepped into view at the kitchen door, holding an apple pie in each hand. After blowing a wisp of hair away from her face, she answered.

"Flyin' an airplane or drivin' a truck, either way, he won't be home much."

It was an answer clearly not intended to merely respond to Chet's question. Then when she noticed his feet up on the table, her eyes squinted like a rifleman taking aim at a coiled rattlesnake.

"And get your feet off the coffee table."

She disappeared back into the kitchen, leaving the boys scrambling to obey. In quick response to her mood swing, Daddy moved his feet off the table and nodded toward Chet's feet, still curled under him on the couch.

He'd married the fiery redhead twelve years ago and, although not highly educated, he was smart enough to recognize her mood swing and the sound of her temper fuse beginning to burn. Those traits were part of her red-headed nature, and Daddy loved the whole package. She was passionate, energetic, and unpredictable. It was those very things that kept their marriage strong and Daddy's mind on her, even when he was on the road for weeks at a time.

"How about we get some pizza?" Daddy called out, anticipating Chet's reaction.

"Yeah ... yeah ... pizza ... pizza!" Chet chanted.

Momma peeked around the kitchen door, looked at them for a few seconds, and then, in a tone of resignation with a half smile on her lips, she answered, "I would like to get out of this kitchen."

Before she had finished speaking, Daddy stood up and Chet climbed onto his back, piggyback style.

"OK. Chet and me'll get cleaned up."

"Pizza ... pizza ... pizza!" Chet continued chanting as he bounced on Daddy's back, mimicking a rodeo cowboy and waving his right hand in circles above his head.

CHAPTER 2

"We need to talk."

Four simple words that hit David Adams like a bucket of ice water dumped on him from behind. Every time. And every time Vivian did it, the frustration of their relational stalemate caused his normally logical and balanced communication skills to teeter dangerously toward a verbal explosion.

He looked up from the book he had been enjoying, closed it, and rested it face down on the inlaid teak side table without making eye contact—not yet. Over their seven-year marriage, he had learned to respond slowly and deliberately to "the talk."

The living room of their contemporary home stood as one the strongest design elements of the twenty-eight-hundred-square-foot, one-story structure. The room spoke in a unique three-dimensional language of shapes, colors, and textures that even the architecturally untrained could somewhat understand.

Less is more.

Form follows function.

All things are by design

Do not compromise.

These phrases offered hints of David's credo regarding life as it should be. Life designed for a purpose. Life empowered by a personal relationship with the creator of all things. Life with a higher purpose than the crumbling world he felt trapped within. Life without compromise.

He slowly moved his slippered feet from the black leather ottoman and rotated in his chair just enough to face her. The leather chair cushions moaned in resistance to his movement, like the sound of chaps rubbing against a saddle. She was semi-reclined on the black leather couch with her back against the padded arm rest and her feet tucked under several frilly throw pillows. Her pillows. She and David had argued over those pillows for weeks until she finally wore him down. Such was her battle with his stubborn ideology.

The moment his eyes met hers, she repeated the statement as if he had not heard it the first time.

"We need to talk."

"OK … talk."

David's tone and facial expression clearly demonstrated his frustration and anticipation of hearing yet more ignorant and misguided get-rich-quick schemes and pathetic excuses for past failures. His architectural practice was slowly dying from the financial drain of her real estate investments and with it their marriage was approaching death by suffocation.

"I have decided to talk to a financial advisor. And David, if we don't do something, we may as well get a divorce."

The distance he felt between himself in the comfortable chair and her on the couch with those stupid frilly pillows strewn about was far greater than the mere eight feet separating them.

"I don't need a financial counselor, Vivian, and I don't want a divorce. What I need is for you to get your rental properties sold and quit bleeding my practice. Maybe then we can redesign this relationship."

He intentionally avoided using the word marriage. His parent's marriage had set the bar, and this was not it. They had been happy together. Even after fifty years. Even to the day they died.

The colors of the setting sun shone through the west-facing living room window which, by design, framed the tree-lined driveway. As Vivian whined on about her life, David gazed through the tall window and watched the blazing fall colors grow dim as the orange glow of the sun slipped below the tree tops.

To divorce would be to fail. To stay married would require compromise. To compromise would be to fail. I prayed. I gave money to the church. God is ignoring me.

Such was David's dilemma.

CHAPTER 3

Thomas Lincoln Winslow sat on the hard, polished wooden pew, fourth row from the front. The Winslow family name was carved on each end of the pew as a symbol of their financial generosity over the years. And, of course, that was where the family sat on Sunday—every Sunday.

Thomas feigned attention as he watched the priest's mouth move, intentionally deaf to the monotone voice of the robed religious icon. His mind was not there in the cold, manmade religious box. As often happens, Thomas was daydreaming—dreaming of a simple and happy life.

His father made millions as a securities broker, but stress and social drinking had alienated him from the family and ultimately caused his death. Thomas was sixteen years old when his father died. The kidney failure was slow, but the liver cancer overtook him quickly and, at the age of forty-seven, he was gone.

Throughout Thomas's life, his father was constantly on business trips or at his offices in New York. And when he was home, he never did "father things" with the children. He always provided plenty of money and toys but never any parenting because that, he believed, was for his wife and the schools to manage.

The family was financially rich—very rich. But Thomas hungered for a different kind of richness. He hungered for the kind of life he could see in the families of some of his friends. Families who came to soccer games. Families with dads who taught sons "guy" things in the garage. Families who ate popcorn and watched television in a real living room. Families who laughed and cried together.

Those activities, unfortunately, did not describe Thomas's family. In his home, the social formalities and obsession with political correctness had created a counterfeit family, one that never looked directly at its members but instead viewed every image and action through the flaw-exposing mirror of social image. And then, of course, there was the all-important perception of the family as judged by others of similar financial status.

Thomas did not know why or how he could see through the phony life that surrounded and controlled him, but he did. And to survive, he learned the value of little white lies and the subtle power of passive aggression. He often used them as self-defense or an escape from a seemingly hopeless future. The feeling of hopelessness always caused him to doubt, to question his ability to survive outside the secure financial umbrella of his family's wealth and the narrow corridor of his mother's control.

The sounds of monotone chanting invaded his senses, and as the voices of the priest, his mother next to him, and the congregation grew louder, his mind slipped back to reality.

… from whom all blessings flow … Praise Father, Son, and Holy Ghost … Amen.

Another Sunday morning was over, and the relief Thomas felt was expressed by a deep sigh as he stood to walk toward the tall, ornately carved wooden doors of the stone-cold building. He walked out of the church and dutifully shook hands with the skinny, effeminate priest who had positioned himself at the door to greet the parishioners as they left.

Thomas's mother followed him out the door and offered her hand to the priest.

"Wonderful message, Father."

To wit, the priest delicately took her hand into his and then nodded as his thin lips morphed into a pious smile. As they walked toward the coffee and tea table that had been set up on the immaculately groomed lawn, Thomas's mother gave her second order of the day. The first was during breakfast, when she demanded that he be on time for the morning service.

"Thomas, you *will* be on time for dinner, I hope," she asked in her typical manner of integrating instructions with anticipated disappointment.

"Yes, Mother. But first I've got to drive over to the airport. I may need to move the plane into the hangar."

The answer was true to form for his well-developed white lie skills. His real reason for going to the airport was to see the vintage World War II airplanes that were flying in for an upcoming air show, and he believed that if she knew the whole truth, there might be a confrontation over the lack of importance of his mission.

"But I will be on time," he obediently promised.

She raised one eyebrow, which signaled her disbelief, and then walked away to gossip with fellow parishioners.

Thomas scanned the parking lot and, for a moment, paused to admire his beautifully restored red 1966 Corvette. He slid his stocky five-foot-eight-inch frame into the classic car and settled into the contoured red and black Recaro racing seat.

The sound of the Corvette's powerful engine, rumbling and awaiting his instructions, injected him with energy and snapped him out of the mental hangover caused by the boring church service. As the mental bondage of the past two hours melted away, his mind was free to lay out the plan for the day.

First the airport ... and then Margie.

When he was safely around the corner from the church, he speed-shifted into second gear and heard the tires squeal beneath him, launching him toward the future.

CHAPTER 4

Chet and Daddy were scrubbed, dressed in clean blue jeans and long-sleeved white shirts, and sitting on the couch with their feet on the floor and their hands on their laps, as though sitting at attention and ready for inspection. Chet was doing his best to mirror Daddy's erect posture and worked hard to hold that pose when Momma came into the room.

She immediately recognized what they were up to and cracked a small smile.

"Good boys."

Her new Levi's fit the way Daddy liked, and her ruffled blouse had a few buttons open at the top.

"All the boys are gonna wish they were me, baby," Daddy said with a wink.

She put her hands on her hips and cocked her head to one side. To Daddy, that looked very sexy, until he heard an unexpected response to his playful words.

"Well, maybe one of them boys'll come over here and fix the shed."

"Fix the shed! Heck no! That busted thing is my reminder of what can happen when I'm backin' box trailers ... I thought you knew that."

Momma looked toward Chet and then back to Daddy.

"We'll talk about it later."

Chet and Momma waited on the front porch while Daddy brought their late-model Ford F-150 pickup truck out of the shed and up the gravel driveway. Momma climbed in, scooted across the bench seat next to Daddy, and patted the seat next to herself.

"Hop in, honey, you get to ride shotgun."

Daddy waited for Chet to get his seatbelt buckled and then drove out of the yard on to the wash-boarded dirt road and headed toward town. Chet watched in the big side-view mirror as the trailing cloud of dust shrouded the house and Daddy's big rig from view.

"Is it hard being a trucker, Daddy?"

"Yes, son, it's hard. It's hard bein' away from you and your momma. It's hard on a person's body … and it's hard to quit once you start."

Then Momma answered the unspoken part of his question.

"You can be a pilot if you want to … heck, you can do anything you put your mind to. Right, Daddy?"

Without taking his eyes off the road, Daddy nodded his head.

"That's right, son. You can do anything you put your mind to."

The pickup turned off the rough dirt road and onto the smooth concrete roadway of Highway 20, heading east toward the Andrews Highway turnoff. The ride to town took them past the southern end of the Midland International Airport and as they passed the airport exit, an American Airlines 727 roared into the sky over the highway ahead. The red and pink colors of the setting sun danced across the highly polished aluminum skin of the fuselage and wings as it aggressively climbed skyward.

"Did you see that?" Chet exclaimed at the awesome sights and sounds.

But the noise of the jet and the wind blowing through the open windows drowned out his words.

The tall neon sign and parking lot of Papa's Pizza Parlor came into view as Daddy exited onto Andrews Highway. Not realizing the tragedy awaiting the young family, he parked under the glowing neon sign and climbed out of the dusty truck onto the parking lot's dirt and gravel surface. As they walked together toward the restaurant, a car leaving the parking lot spun its tires, creating a billowing cloud of dust that drifted across their path and enveloped them. Chet sneezed and coughed as the dust invaded his throat and eyes. Daddy heard him cough and saw him rubbing his eyes as the offending dust cloud slowly moved passed. He pulled a red shop rag out of his pocket and leaned down to wipe a matting of moist dirt near his eyes.

"Don't let that stuff choke you, son … spit it out."

Momma brushed Chet's hair with her fingers. "Let's get inside."

The painted wooden door to the restaurant had a window in the top half and a red-and-white checkered curtain hung on the inside. The blood-red paint was chipped near the worn brass doorknob, and the chipped areas revealed the underlying layers of the old building's colorful history. It had been built in the early 1950s as a two-story farmhouse. Then, twenty years later when Andrews Highway was expanded to a four-lane expressway, it was converted into a bar and grill called Hank's Roadhouse. There had been rumors that the second floor was a brothel, but nobody could ever prove it. After a six-year run, the bar and grill (and likely brothel) closed down. The building stood empty and in disrepair for a few years, but as the city of Midland grew, it was cleaned up, painted red, and became Papa's Pizza Parlor.

Daddy pushed the door open and held it there for Chet and Momma. They were greeted by a waitress in a ruffled white dress with a red-and-white checkered apron that matched the door curtain and the tablecloths. Except for the tray of beer bottles balanced on her left hand, she looked like she was dressed up for a square dance.

She pointed to a nearby table.

"Somebody'll be right with you."

The only other waitress working that night approached and asked in a thick Texas accent, "Y'all ready to order?"

"Yeah, let's have a medium The Works, a Dr. Pepper, and two Longnecks."

Chet loved it when Daddy ordered because it was the only time Momma would let him have a Dr. Pepper. Too much sugar, she always said.

Not counting the waitresses, there were only five other people in the restaurant, and when their waitress brought out the drink order, Daddy asked, "Slow night?"

"Yeah, Tuesday nights usually are," she answered and then disappeared into the kitchen.

About twenty minutes later, she re-appeared with their steaming-hot pizza, which prompted Momma to place paper napkins around the table.

Daddy reached out and took Momma's and Chet's hands into his.

"Son, would you say the blessing for us?"

"OK … Dear God, thanks for the pizza … amen."

Daddy and Momma looked at each other and smiled, which was their way of saying "Isn't he cute?" without him hearing it.

Then Daddy released their hands and announced, "Let's eat."

Chet would have loved to tell Daddy all about school and ask him about the things he saw on his trip, but the pizza was too good and his mouth was full. Momma did not like it when he talked with his mouth full.

Daddy did not talk much either. In fact, Daddy could not talk at all. Instead, he was holding his throat with his left hand and reaching for Momma with his right. His face was blue and his eyes were rolling back as she turned toward him. She screamed for help and grabbed his shirtsleeve but could not hold him as he fell sideways off the bench onto the sawdust-covered floor.

The people in the dining room heard Momma's scream and came rushing to see. Some of them knelt down near Daddy and tried to help, but none of them could get his breath back.

An ambulance came and took him away.

CHAPTER 5

"David Scott Adams, the court has reviewed your rebuttal to the divorce action filed on behalf of Vivian Leslie Adams and finds in favor of the plaintiff."

Then the judge looked directly at David and his attorney and ceremoniously dropped the gavel. The abrupt sound of the wood gavel as it struck the bench echoed throughout the old courtroom.

"Divorce granted."

The judge signaled for the bailiff to approach the bench and passed the documents that David's attorney would need to finalize the divorce settlement.

"Dave, I'm sorry. We tried. Do you still want to file for Chapter Seven bankruptcy or would you like me to negotiate a Chapter Thirteen for you?"

The trim, middle-aged attorney looked straight into David's eyes and awaited his instructions. For a few seconds, David did not speak as he watched his newly estranged wife and her attorney walk out of the courtroom together.

"No, I'm done. I'm done … Screw it. I'm done. Chapter Seven clears the table, right? They lose, I win."

"Well, yes, sort of. The IRS still has to be paid. But other than that, you'd be free of all debt."

That was all David needed to know. As he balanced the pros and cons, he realized that he was making the decision alone—

completely alone. There was no one else to ask, no one else to convince, and no Vivian there to point an accusing finger at him if he made the wrong decision. The strength and conviction of his newly found autonomy spoke through him.

"Do it, I'm done."

The attorney reached out and offered a sympathetic handshake.

"I'll get you the bankruptcy paperwork to sign within the week. Good luck, Mr. Adams."

David did not hear the words or see the gesture.

The attorney simply nodded, pick up his briefcase, and left David alone in the emptying courtroom. The only sound David heard was the hissing of the ancient hydraulic door closer as the heavy oak door to the judge's chambers slowly pulled shut. The faint sound floated through the air and then faded away like the last breath of a dying man.

He was forty-two years old, trim, and of average height. But his appearance and demeanor were much more youthful, in part because of jet black, straight hair and an almost beardless face. Somewhere in his ancestral past, a Comanche Indian blood line brought dark hair, light beards, and an almost tan skin color into his European, Caucasian family line. To some people, the idea of looking younger than his or her age would be a blessing, but to David, it had been a curse. To him, it seemed that whatever he did, there was always someone with more credibility or more articulate speaking skills, or someone older who, because of wrinkles or gray hair, was perceived as having more authority.

Denial and anger ripped through David's mind in an emotional competition for control and from it thoughts and questions fell onto his heart.

This shouldn't be happening. My father was a respected lawyer and judge. My mom and dad stuck it out. They died happy and old. What in hell did I do to deserve this?

In preparation for the chilly walk to his car, he pulled on a tan London Fog trench coat and brown leather gloves. He took his time with each glove and verbalized the mental and spiritual combat within, spitting the words.

"Does it really matter? Do I really care? I thought God had a plan for my life. Where is He in all this?"

He walked through the courthouse lobby to the exit and as he pushed on the wooden double doors, a gust of cold wind pulled them open as if to say "Now get out!"

The concrete steps and sidewalks had been sprinkled with salt to melt the snow and ice. As he slowly walked to his car, David kept his gaze downward. The footprints he left in the salty slush slowly fill with dirty water from the street. Halfway to his car, he felt the winter-laden afternoon wind invade his trench coat, sending a mild chill through his body. He mumbled to the ground as he neared the protection of his car.

"Well, God, I'm done. I prayed, I gave money, I went to church and this is it. Nothing. I'm done. I'm done with you."

Looking down as he was, David did not see the new, white Ford Taurus pull into the courthouse parking lot and park a few spaces away. The whiteness and puffy shape of that particular model gave it a lumpy marshmallow look and when the driver squeezed out of the car, the image was complete. He could easily have doubled for the Pillsbury Doughboy in a tight-fitting gray business suit and vest that strained to contain his ample belly.

The voice of the pudgy preacher pierced David's emotional tirade.

"David! David! I'm sorry. Am I late? Some people just don't know how to drive in snow."

"Yeah, it's over."

"Oh, I'm so sorry."

The preacher turned and pointed to a nearby cafe.

"Can we get some coffee and talk about it?"

For a moment, David studied the short, rotund man. His blow-dried hair was combed back and held in place with ample coats of hairspray, and his pasty white complexion was blotched with reddish patches where the cold wind blew across his chubby cheeks and chin.

Although David felt the preacher was as much at fault as God, he managed a somewhat respectful response.

"No. No time. I've got a lot to do. I got to go."

"OK, I understand. See you at church tonight?"

David turned and walked the short distance to his car, leaving the preacher unsure of how to respond to the intentionally rude body language. Then David opened the car door, climbed in, and just before pulling it closed, he tossed a bitter response over his shoulder.

"Not likely!"

His life, marriage, and career had taken paths that can be symbolically described as riding a roller coaster at Six Flags over Texas, with all the ups, downs, twists, turns, and one final climb to the summit that invariably ends in a careening downward plunge.

As David drove away, he watched the familiar Tulsa streets and the dumbfounded preacher grow smaller and smaller in the rearview mirror of his soon-to-be-repossessed Cadillac Seville. The shrinking images in the mirror symbolized the demise of a failed life he was determined to leave behind. The determination continued to grow, and he clung to it like an anchor in an angry sea until finally it matured into rock-solid resolve.

"Get on with my life. Life without financial hassles. Life without Vivian."

After a pause that lasted two deep breaths, he said, "Without God."

As he spoke aloud to himself and the windshield, a ray of sunshine broke through the overcast sky off to the west.

"Maybe I'll go to California."

When he glanced at the dashboard to check his speed, the odometer caught his eye: 8,888.8.

New beginnings.

CHAPTER 6

The funeral service was held in the same little country church where Momma and Daddy had been married twelve years earlier. She sat in the front pew with Chet sitting as close to her as he could manage.

Although the organist was playing a mournful dirge and people were making their way toward their seats, Momma's mind and heart were deaf to the sounds. Tears blurred her vision as she sat staring at the simple wooden casket resting on a chrome gurney next to the preacher's podium and the worn oak altar—the same altar she and Daddy had knelt on when they went forward together to accept Jesus as their Lord and Savior.

The preacher had told her it would be best if Chet went forward with her to view the open casket. He said something about closure, which she did not understand but nevertheless agreed to follow his instructions.

When the preacher had finished and Daddy's friends who wanted to say a few words were done, the preacher nodded at Momma, indicating it was time to come forward with Chet and begin the formal viewing. She took Chet's hand in hers, and they slowly approached the casket.

Standing on his tiptoes, Chet was tall enough to see over the edge of the casket and after a quick peek, he looked up at his Momma, surprised, and whispered.

"That's not Daddy."

Momma heard his whisper and, without looking away from the closed eyes of the cosmetically masked corpse, she whispered back.

"I know, honey."

Then choking on her words she struggled to finish.

"Daddy's in heaven."

———

Three days after the funeral, a seemingly innocent event occurred that would impact the remainder of Chet's life. Momma's friends had come over to the house, brought food, and helped with laundry and house cleaning. And some of Daddy's friends did the yard chores and even fixed the shed.

One of Daddy's trucker friends had come over to get the red Freightliner and felt the urge to look in on Chet. With Momma's permission, he knocked on the bedroom door and, after waiting a few seconds, walked into the semi-dark room. Chet was in bed, curled up in a fetal position under his Roy Rogers blanket.

The burly trucker carefully stepped over the toy cars and airplanes strewn around the floor and knelt down, resting on the heels of his boots. He spoke as softly as he could and, in the gravelly voice of a longtime smoker, whispered, "I'm sorry about your Daddy, son. He was good people."

Then, after patting Chet on the top of the head, he turned to leave the room but paused at the door.

"I don't know why bad things happen to good people … I'm real sorry."

A few minutes later, Momma came into Chet's room and sat down on the bed.

"Honey, you've got to eat something. Come on into the kitchen and have some supper."

Before Chet could answer, the sound of Daddy's truck starting up filled the room and, for a brief moment, both Chet and Momma felt the familiar rush of emotions brought on by the sound of the big rig.

Then, slowly, the bitter reality of death returned and in their broken hearts they knew that this time the sound meant goodbye. This time Daddy was not in the cab waving his red shop rag at them as he pulled away. Chet climbed out of bed and walked with Momma to the bedroom window. They stood and watched in silence as the big red tractor and flatbed trailer pulled out from the spot where Daddy had parked it. In just a few minutes, it slipped away, down the country road and out of sight, shrouded in dust.

Chet broke the silence.

"Momma, what are we gonna do now?"

She looked down at his upturned face and into his sad blue eyes.

"I don't know, honey ... maybe we'll move."

"Where?" he asked with his eyes locked onto hers.

She looked out the window for a moment and then turned back to Chet.

"Daddy always talked about going to California someday."

At first, Chet just looked up at her and then, to her surprise, he asked a question totally unrelated to the conversation. He asked the question that would keep him mentally separated from God for years to come.

"Momma, why do bad things happen to good people?"

She was unable to respond with words but instead kissed his freckled forehead. And the tear that followed the kiss fell onto his upturned face.

CHAPTER 7

As was customary every Sunday, the Winslow family gathered at Mother's house for dinner around the stately mahogany table set with the best china, polished silver, and fresh-cut flowers. The dining room was the centerpiece of the sprawling California Spanish home, in part because Mrs. Winslow enjoyed entertaining and hosting fund-raising dinners for the underprivileged, but also because the large arched windows provided impressive views of the Laguna Beach coastline.

With their meal, the family engaged in conversation that was offered as if highly significant but was, in truth, petty gossip. Thomas sat at the foot of the table as usual, watching and listening politely, hoping to be ignored. But as often happened, his Yale-educated and overconfident older brother turned the conversation onto him.

"So Tom, what are you going to do? You can't live here with Mother forever."

"Yes he can!" snapped Thomas's teenaged little sister with all the spoiled brat tone she could muster.

Mother intervened, as she always felt the need to do.

"Thomas, your brother is right. You really must decide what you are going to do with your life. And I certainly hope it doesn't include that girl you've been seeing. She is not good enough for you. Isn't her father a laborer or something?"

The redness of Thomas's face betrayed his relatively calm tone of voice.

"Her father is a contractor. I'm not dating her father, for God's sake, I'm dating her. And yes, I intend to move out within the month. I have been offered a job with the FAA in San Diego."

"Wow!" exclaimed his sister. "Will you be a spy or a presidential bodyguard?"

The humor of her immature and ignorant question eased the stress around the table, allowing Thomas to respond in a relaxed, almost parental tone.

"FAA, honey, not CIA. It stands for Federal Aviation Administration. I'll be evaluating training manuals for pilots and hopefully work my way up to examiner someday."

Thomas's brother picked up a crystal water goblet and interrupted. "Well, it's a start I guess."

Then he pushed his chair back, stood at the head of the table, and held the goblet in the air. After a glance around the room to confirm that all eyes were on him, he cleared his throat and turned on his overdone toastmaster's voice.

"And now, I propose a toast!"

Thomas looked away and gazed through the tall arched windows. His eyes focused on the almost invisible line of the horizon as it blended the ocean's edge with the hazy afternoon sky. Then, taking a deep breath, he mumbled that which he knew he could not say aloud.

"Sarcastic bastard."

He felt relieved that he got away with saying those words without getting caught. But the relief was nothing compared to the release he felt for having finally stood his ground about Margie. After a few minutes, he dutifully turned his attention back to the family gathering, where the table conversation had predictably moved on to matters of little importance and a thought began rolling over and over in his mind.

There has to be more to life than this. There has to be.

The hypnotic mental escape continued until the sights and sounds of the dining room finally faded away and visions of a new life took their place. His brother's toast to family and money went unheard, and his mother's instructions that everyone move to the veranda for dessert was ignored. He had disappeared again into the fantasy world of life with Margie and a new beginning—a beginning he could almost touch.

CHAPTER 8

David was free. The furniture was auctioned off, the house and cars repossessed, and his Tulsa office closed. When he finally headed to California, his sole possessions were a five-year-old Chevrolet Malibu purchased from a used car lot that advertised "no credit, no problem"; a box of drafting tools; some photo albums; his clothes; and the gift of financial freedom that shined like the silver lining of a departing storm.

For him, it seemed the worst was over. He had rebuilt his life from the debris without the burdensome advice of a spouse or God and without praying or waiting for some "could be God" answer.

Owing to what he believed were a few lucky breaks, his piece of the construction market had proven easier to grab than he expected. He had landed three projects with a condominium developer, two custom-built home clients, a warehouse project in Las Vegas, and an affordable office in San Diego's Old Town.

As part of his commission for the condominium projects, David agreed to accept the title for two of the units. In the years to come, he would acquire a great deal of property in the same manner and for a purpose not yet revealed to him. But until then, David lived in a modest, furnished apartment overlooking Mission Bay.

The steaming spray stung his shoulders and knees as he sat naked in the dark, huddled in the corner of the shower enclosure with his head slumped down and hoping the guilt and fear would wash away. His head hurt. His eyes burned. His stomach was sour. His tongue felt like sandpaper. But more daunting than those discomforts, he did not know her name, only that she had spent the night.

He had gone to happy hour at one of his favorite bars and hooked up with a group of tourists from a Los Angeles-to-Cabo San Lucas cruise ship docked downtown. When he came to, he found the used condom wrapped in tissue lying on the floor next to the bed and the scent of a woman on the sheets. He did not remember much about last night except offering to buy the fifth round of tequila shots and Corona chasers. It was part of the "work all week and party on the weekend" cycle David found himself addicted to—that and a growing need for a couple drinks every night to relax before bed. His raspy whisper was lost in the splattering sounds of the shower.

"Why in hell do I do this to myself?"

Then, because of the pain inflected by the sound of his own voice and the discomfort of the water rushing over his face, he slowly pulled himself up. He stood with his back against the steaming downpour and pressed his hands against the tile wall in front of him.

The self-imposed mental interrogation continued. *What have I done? Who was she? When did she leave? Did the condom work? Damn it! Damn it!*

One hour and three cups of coffee later, he was dressed and driving to the office as the responsibilities of the day overshadowed the guilt-filled reality of morning.

CHAPTER 9

The heavily loaded U-Haul truck rumbled west on Interstate 10. If she could keep up the sixty mile per hour average speed, they would be in Tucson, Arizona, by 7:30 p.m. Chet rode with his right arm sticking out of the window and watched the wind move his hand up and down as he rotated his wrist.

"Momma! Watch this!" he shouted over the noise of the rushing wind. "My hand can fly like an airplane."

She kept her eyes on the road and, with both hands firmly gripping the steering wheel, she glanced at the big side mirrors.

"OK, but be careful, honey."

Although she heard Chet and answered, her mind was far away. The struggle to sell the house and leave her friends was more difficult than she ever imagined, and a guilty feeling for moving so far away from the cemetery where her husband was laid to rest haunted her. But in her heart, she knew they were doing the right thing. There were too many painful memories in that old house, and Chet needed a chance to experience the world beyond the little Texas town.

Chet had closed the passenger window and moved to the middle of the bench seat next to her. She glanced down and brushed dust off the knees of his new Levis.

"It's gonna get dark soon. We'll find a place to stay when we get to Tucson."

She pointed to his lap, and he obeyed the silent instructions by putting on the seat belt.

"Where is El Cajon, Momma?"

"It's in California, close to San Diego and the ocean."

"Is San Diego in America?"

Momma giggled and looked toward him for a moment and then answered.

"Well, yes, silly. Didn't they teach you anything at that school?"

Just before the last word slid past her lips, she recognized the subtle insult attached to her question.

"When we get to Tucson, I'll show you where California, San Diego, and El Cajon are on the big road atlas, OK?"

Chet could see the big map book resting on the dashboard.

They rode on in silence. Momma hoped the apartment was clean and ready for them to move in, and Chet daydreamed about flying.

CHAPTER 10

Financial recovery and success came to David Adams, but peace and fulfillment evaded him. Every success, every new client, everything he believed would fill the emptiness deep within his soul had failed. Nothing he had accomplished filled the void. Nothing satisfied it—not the money, not the architectural projects, not the cars, not the booze, not the women. Nothing.

And the nights were torture.

The escape of sleep teased but refused to come until the noises in his head subsided. He struggled to fall asleep as the events of the day and plans for tomorrow poured over him like falling pieces of a spilled puzzle. And the mental flood continued until his conscious mind was finally spent, leaving his subconscious to continue the battle in dreams. Dreams that played confusing, jumbled, nonsensical dramas awakening him in the hours of darkness.

But on a Saturday night, Easter eve, a new and radically different dream took him. That night, he fell into a dream that initiated his spiritual healing and prepared him for a unique and secret plan soon to be revealed. A soft, cool breeze laden with the scent of ocean air drifted through the open bedroom window as David lay under only a bed sheet with several pillows nestled around him. His mind was spent, and he finally drifted to sleep just as the sounds of someone entering the condominium courtyard two floors below floated into his room.

Undisturbed by the sounds, David dreamt.

The dark, narrow alley was strewn with filthy debris and saturated with the stench of death. Deformed human-shaped figures lurked in nearby shadows on his left. And on his right, he saw a vine-covered wall. In the wall, partially hidden by tangled vines, was a gate. He cautiously stepped over the waste and decaying debris lying in his path. As he moved closer, he noticed a rusty metal latch partially hidden but reachable. He pulled the vines away and slid open the latch.

Then, pushing on the gate with his shoulder, he slowly forced it to move. As it surrendered to his effort, the vines stretched and finally broke, like pulling apart a giant spider web. Shoulder first, he squeezed through. The gate closed silently behind him, separating and protecting him from the lost world he had escaped.

In this new and wonderful place, the sweet warm air embraced him with scents of flowers and damp grass that covered the rolling hills between him and the distant mountains. The visual pull of the mountains and the sounds of gurgling water that flowed in a nearby brook beckoned, like the open arms of a nurturing mother to her child.

When he reached the brook, he sat down on the soft grassy surface and surrendered to the peace that surrounded him. As he lay back, he sank a few inches into the grass. His unspoken thoughts affirmed the healing peace that filled the place and feelings of perfect love flooded over him. He was unafraid and secure, sensing the protective love of his heavenly Father and enjoying an inner warmth like that of a child cradled snuggly at his mother's breasts.

Nearby, a white robed figure stood leaning casually against one of the large trees that ran along the opposite edge of the brook. David was aware of His presence and an odd mixture of fear and joy gripped him as the robed figure walked across the water toward hm. As He got closer, the fear subsided and feelings of happiness, childlike and wonderful, came over David as he recognized the robed man.

"Jesus?"

Now standing at David's feet, Jesus looked down at him and then did a strange yet wonderful thing. Without speaking, He lay down on the grass beside David and positioned Himself exactly into the same position and posture as David. For a few minutes, they lay in audible silence, yet David heard these truths spoken to his heart.

Nothing you have done, no pain you have experienced, no anger you have tasted, no guilt you have felt, no sadness you have suffered … Nothing will separate you from Me. I paid the price and you are free. I Am in you and you are in Me.

The words flowed into the void of David's heart, the void his temporal world could not fill, freeing him and at the same time strengthening him with a lost yet familiar spiritual energy.

Jesus stood and as He did, David rose with Him. Then, standing face to face, David saw Jesus look toward the grass where they had lain. David's eyes followed and there he saw the symbol of Jesus' words. Impressed in the grass were two imprints, side by side and exactly, precisely, incomprehensibly the same. As if made by the same person.

As he stood there face to face with Jesus, bathed in the brilliant light that radiated from His robe, a soft humming sound surrounded him. Then Jesus reached out and placed his hands on David's shoulders.

"I will empower you … I will lead you … prove Me."

The humming increased until David was awakened. The alarm clock next to his bed buzzed loudly as the digital numbers flashed 5:55 a.m. God's grace.

CHAPTER 11

David's dream had filled his mind and heart with an urging, a calling to reconnect his spirit with God.

At first, he resisted. The very thought of going to church touched the scars of the past, awakening the sadness of failures and the frustration of unresolved anger. The booze and illicit intimacy with women of long-forgotten faces and names had temporarily soothed his pain. But God's reality exposed the Devil's lies.

Miraculously, his heart finally overpowered the wall his mind and emotions had so efficiently constructed between him and God. But the fear of failure and a lingering disdain of church buildings and preachers lay in his path, like the rubble of a collapsed barrier that must be crossed with caution and risk of injury.

He found a church where he believed he could be lost in a crowd of several thousand people and sat near the back of the expansive auditorium. His emotions wanted him to be invisible and his mind wanted him to bolt for the door. But his heart was rekindled with memories of how it felt to be right with God and how grateful he was that Jesus died for his sins—all of his sins.

The service ended, and people began to leave and mingle. David slipped down to the front and stood before the big cross mounted on the wall and waited, hoping to sense God's presence. Although several people stood nearby, God supernaturally protected him from unwanted human distraction. When he looked down at the red carpeted floor, his eyes and mind saw carpet, but his spirit revealed a different image: blood. Christ's blood.

His mind and emotions felt joy and relief and his spirit saw guilt and sin falling off his body into the blood at his feet. Then came the old and familiar feelings of relational confidence, peace, and God's love that he once knew. He felt the evidence of God's presence kindling within him and as he opened his heart, Jesus moved closer and closer to him. Empowering him. Freeing him.

The wonder of it took his breath away in short gasps until finally his heart was so full that his body and mind could not contain it. Tears blurred his vision. He closed his eyes and breathed deeply, to fill, to purge, and finally to talk to God like a frightened child to a loving parent.

"Lord, I want You back in my life, but I don't trust You. I can't survive another mess like that. You didn't prevent it last time. Why should I believe that You would protect me this time?"

Sometimes answers to prayer come as feelings and other times as an audible voice. The answer David heard was a soft clear voice, as though the words were spoken by someone standing nearby. And what he heard permanently healed the scars and began the plan God had for him.

You did what you wanted to do. I never left you. I Am with you then. I Am with you now. I Am with you in the future. Prove Me.

David dropped to his knees and lowered his face into the palms of his hands.

A man's hand rested gently on his right shoulder followed by a new voice, the voice of a man kneeling beside him.

"You are complete in Jesus. His way is your way. His truth is your truth. And your life is His. God has a Scripture for you."

Without looking up, David simply nodded. He could hear the crackle of pages being turned but still did not look up. The gentle voice continued.

"John 14:6: I am the way and the truth and the life. No one comes to the Father except through me."

The hand lifted from David's shoulder, and he looked up to see a tall slender man smiling down at him.

"My name is Matthew Solman, and I believe God has a plan that includes the both of us."

Matthew nodded toward a nearby pew and they sat down. The inner calmness of David's heart showed in his relaxed demeanor and the softness in his eyes as he listened to Matthew's story.

"Three years ago, God put a plan on my heart ... no, more of a challenge. You see, I am an accountant, and numbers mean more to me than to others. For example, as I stood behind you at the altar, God placed John 14:6 on my heart."

David leaned forward slightly and nodded but did not speak.

"God has shown me that, when guided by His Holy Spirit, numbers sometimes have deeper meanings. Meanings that can reveal more about the words or events they relate to. And the Scripture John 14:6 has multilevel significance."

He paused and wrote the Scripture on a small notepad he pulled from his shirt pocket.

"Notice that if I simply add one to the six in the verse, it becomes seven. Also notice that fourteen simply divided becomes two sevens."

Matthew looked up from the notepad and waited for a response from David.

"Go ahead, I follow you so far."

"OK. In the study of Biblical numerology, seven means completion or perfection, and six is the number for man. In the case of John 14:6, we can use the numbers to reveal more about the Scripture as it relates to you and me."

He wrote a simple formula on the notepad and held it up for David to see: John 14:6 = 7 + 7 : (6+1) = 777

"So, David, can you see?"

"Yes. I am complete when Jesus is in me."

Matthew smiled, nodded, and continued.

"And three sevens are significant. The number three represents the Triune Godhead: Father, Son, and Holy Spirit. With Jesus added to your life, you become a child of the Trinity."

He paused again and then continued.

"But there is more. Remember, David, the numeric analysis adds depth to the written word. God not only gave me that Scripture for you but also gave me words for you. Can you recall them?"

David looked up and spoke like a student reciting from memory.

"I am complete in Jesus. His way is my way. His truth is my truth. And my life is His."

Matthew smiled warmly.

"And yet there is more."

"More?"

"Yes. A way is a planned route, a path that God has been preparing you for. And David, I believe it is a plan that we are to take on together. Before I tell you more, I must ask, what is your profession?"

CIRCA AD 2001

CHAPTER 12

David Adams stood near Runway 27 Left with his fingers entwined in the airport chain link perimeter fence watching small planes touch and go and talking to God.

Fifteen years had passed since his spiritual recovery and his association with Matthew Solman. He was a few pounds heavier but not overweight for his age and still looked healthy in the right clothes. His hair was trimmed short and had turned white close to his ears.

It's strange how I've been drawn to this little airport. How can I justify this? My work schedule is insane. How can I find the time? But here I am again, Lord. What should I do?

A little Cessna 152 turned onto final and drifted toward the earth. It bobbed and wobbled as it floated toward the pavement, finally dropping onto the runway only to bounce a foot or so back into the air before agreeing to land.

David judged the landing.

I can do better than that.

CHAPTER 13

The offices of the San Diego FAA were starkly institutional and, as often occurred in bureaucratic agencies, the interior suffered from a compromising process known as "design by committee." Although the dull yellow color was intended to be inoffensive and soothing to the human eye, over a decade had past. Now the building's paint was faded, stained, and grimy at places, like doorjambs, wall corners, and light switches. On the floor, the medium gray-colored sheet vinyl was marred with permanent scuffs partially hidden beneath layers of old floor wax.

Each office was the same size and accessed through a gray metal door with a twelve-inch by twelve-inch safety glass window installed at adult eye level. The few exceptions were the offices of the department heads. Because of their positions in the bureaucratic pecking order, they got slightly larger offices with somewhat newer furniture and usually a window or two.

A small office directly across the hall from one of the department heads had a brown laminated nameplate attached to the wall next to the door and on it the name Thomas Winslow was inscribed in white block letters.

A short distance down the hall, in the communal kitchen, Tom was sitting alone, pondering his future. He was on a fifteen-minute coffee break as scheduled and religiously followed by everyone in his department.

Over the years, he had kept the same stocky, barrel chest football player physique. But his hair, which was thinning when he married Margie, was almost gone from the crown of his head, and the combover he managed to create every morning grew lower and closer to his left ear. He rubbed his temples and forehead with his finger tips, the way Margie did when she gave him rubdowns. With a deep sigh, he confessed.

"This isn't it. This is not what I want to do the rest of my life."

Over the complaints of his family, Tom had married the girl that they had said "wasn't good enough for him." He loved her and their house in the suburbs and cherished their nine years of marriage. There was nothing Tom would do to change that part of his life. Neither would he change his side job, his hobby, flying. He had logged over two thousand flying hours giving lessons in the flying club beaters at Montgomery Field and in his Piper Seneca.

But his position with the FAA had stalled, and there was nothing he would rather do than escape the bureaucratic box he found himself trapped within. His frustrated reflection was interrupted by a coworker.

"Tom, Mac is looking for you. I told him you were on break."

Earl McSwain, nicknamed "Mac," was an FAA inspector and head of Tom's department. His ego and greed for power deluded him into believing that the nickname Mac enhanced his employee-to-subordinate relationship. But in truth, he was not trusted and most assuredly not popular. He had earned the employee's distrust by his slippery management style and a history of using people to work his way up through the system. For him, the job was just a stepping stone on the way to a position in Washington, DC, where his professional fantasy placed him in an important role with the National Transportation Safety Board, the NTSB.

Tom tapped on the doorjamb of Mac's open office door.
"You wanted to see me?"

Mac looked up and blinked, appearing somewhat startled by the interruption.

"Tom. Yeah, come on in. Close the door and have a seat."

As Tom approached, Mac slipped a pornographic magazine he had been ogling from his lap into the open side drawer of his desk, hoping it had not been noticed. Tom sat in one of the two metal chairs across the desk from the paunchy, square-jawed department head. It was common office knowledge that the short little man carried a huge Napoleon complex. Knowing that prompted Tom to wait for him to speak first.

Mac looked down at his desk and tapped a yellow pencil on the desktop. Then he ceremoniously cleared his throat and looked up at Tom.

"I know you've been looking for a chance to move up to an inspector position. I haven't forgotten you. I called you in here because there may be something opening up in about three months. If you're still interested, I'll see what I can do to get you on."

The surprise and timing of the opportunity dropping into his lap caused Tom to stand up, almost jumping to his feet.

"Yes. Yes, you bet. I'll get my personnel file updated and start the paperwork. Thank you, Mac."

Mac held his hands up in a surrendering humble fashion.

"No problem. Glad to do what I can."

As he left the office, Tom turned to give a parting thank you, but found Mac leaning back in his chair, facing the office window and talking on the telephone. He rushed to his office to call Margie with the good news. What he did not know was that Mac was offering the same inspector position to another employee, one who possibly had a friend in the NTSB. Mac would work it to his advantage because he always did.

CHAPTER 14

The Gillespie Field Flight School shared a one-story building with the airport café and a maintenance hangar, located in the shadow of the control tower. The buildings were constructed in the 1960s and the paint finish, the doors, and the windows appeared to have been recently redone.

As David entered the lobby, two young men wearing white flight school shirts and carrying small chart cases walked toward him with a determined step in their stride. They crossed paths with him on their way to the glass doors leading out to the ramp, where several very used single engine airplanes were tied down.

"Excuse me, pop," one of them said as he brushed past toward the door.

David did not speak, but his eyes dressed him down like a drill sergeant preparing to bring some boot camp reality to a new recruit.

Pop! Great. Now I'm the old guy.

The way the word "pop" hit David surprised him. He thought the lack of respect issues were resolved, but apparently not, because more choice responses were forming in his head. It took all his willpower to stifle the temptation to fire the responses at the young men as they exited to the ramp. He was frustrated, angry, and ready to leave when a voice called from an open office door behind him.

"Can I help you?"

"Yeah," David responded, not intending to sound as irritated as he felt.

He walked into the office and found a skinny guy dressed like he picked his clothes out of a dirty laundry basket. The guy was sitting behind an old and unbelievably cluttered desk. After a quick look around the room, David finished the response.

"I'm curious about what it takes to get flight lessons. You know, time and money."

The skinny guy smiled, offered David a seat, and somehow found an application form buried in the desktop pileup.

"Just fill this out and we can get an idea of what you need."

"Thanks, I'll do it at home and come back by in a couple days."

The quick response was driven by anxiety that was building inside him and the lingering emotions left over from the mental battle he just fought in the lobby.

The skinny guy turned in his chair and looked at a calendar hanging on the wall next to his desk.

"OK, how about tomorrow around two? I'll have one of my flight instructors here to meet with you. He can tell you more about how long it'll take than I can."

As he was speaking, David heard the grinding, whining sounds of an engine starting, followed by the muffled roar and whirling resonance unique to piston engine airplanes. The sounds provided a filter for his mind, a filter that washed away lingering memories of life's past failures.

"You know, two o'clock tomorrow works for me. I'll see you then."

He walked through the lobby and breathed in the smell of airplane exhaust fumes.

Airport smells. I like it.

After pausing to watch a twin-engine Piper Seneca take off, he climbed into his car and headed to the office. Westbound

FLIGHT *to the* PROMISE

Interstate 8 was congested, and as he worked his way through the traffic, he made a cell phone call. There was no answer. He left a message on the machine.

"This is Dave. How do my accounts receivable and line look? I'm thinking of buying an airplane. Call me in the next couple days. Thanks."

Before David got to the parking lot at his office, the hands-free phone in his car rang.

"Dave. Got your message. What are you up to now?"

"Matt! Thanks for getting back so quickly. Did you already look at my money situation?"

"Yeah, you look great. The line of credit is down to less than one hundred thousand, your cash flow is strong, and receivables are still holding at about 3 million. I wish we could get that down. But you look really good."

Before the "What are you up to?" question could be asked again, David jumped in.

"I may start flying lessons tomorrow. And maybe, just maybe, I'll buy an airplane for business travel. Time will tell. I just needed to know how to approach it. I won't do anything without getting you on board first."

"Promise?"

"Yup, I promise. I'll call you tomorrow."

David pressed the disconnect button.

Matt was the Matthew Solman who met David at the altar on the Easter Sunday of his spiritual recovery. And in their divinely guided relationship, they worked together on a secret plan that God laid before them as the precarious future of religious freedom crept closer.

David understood that most of life's challenges were due to spiritual strongholds surrounding worldly circumstances. There were three million dollars out there that his company had honestly earned, and two million of it was past due. His confidence and love for God, and the knowledge he retained from the Bible regarding spiritual battles, led him to know exactly what to do when he hit a stronghold. He was a child of the King and with the power of the Holy Spirit, he could see beyond the limitations of the world, men, and mere financial setbacks. David also knew that spiritual powers were at work doing whatever they could to screw up the lives of God's children.

He pulled into the reserved parking space at the base of his office building and shut off the engine. No one was around nor could anyone see him through the tinted windows of his late-model Mercedes sedan. He opened his heart and prayed.

"Father, I love You and I want only Your will in my life. With Your permission and with the power and authority of Jesus' name, I order all demonic powers, principalities, and ungodly spiritual beings to get away from the money that is rightfully mine. Now Father, I stand in faith and believe that Your will is free to move forward in my life. I stand and believe that You and You alone will show me the way and use me for Your purposes. Thank You, Father. In Jesus's name, thank You."

CHAPTER 15

A warm breeze drifted across the tarmac carrying with it the sounds of a Piper Cherokee at full throttle, rolling for takeoff. David walked from his car and across the parking lot toward the Gillespie Field Flight School with a completed application gripped tightly in his right hand. As he walked through the doorway, he heard a somewhat familiar voice.

"I never got your name, but I'm glad you made it back."

He looked in the direction of the voice and saw the skinny guy sitting on the lobby couch just as disheveled and wearing what appeared to be yesterday's shirt. Sitting on the other end of the couch was a lanky young man who looked to be in his early twenties, wearing a starched long-sleeved white shirt, faded blue jeans, and a red baseball cap with CAL POLY/SLO emblazoned above the brim. His red hair competed with the color of the cap.

Upon making eye contact with David, the tall young man immediately stood and held out his hand.

"My name is Chet Rawlins. Glad to meet you," he stated with a slight Southern drawl.

David returned the gesture and shook his hand.

"David … David Adams, but call me Dave. Good to meet you."

"I understand you want flight lessons?"

"Yeah, if I'm not too old," David confessed.

"Well, you're not. Let's see your application."

Chet reached out for the form still gripped tightly David's hand. As David surrendered the application, something that felt more like a prayer than a thought floated through his mind.

God, I'm really doing this!

Chet quickly glanced at the application.

"Let me tell you a little about myself and then you can tell me why you want to fly. Deal?"

"Deal."

Chet sat back down on the couch, and David pulled up the overstuffed chair next to the couch. As soon as both men were seated, the skinny guy stood up, looked down at them, and focused on David.

"When you're done, come into my office so we can do the rest of the paperwork."

As the skinny guy spoke, he rubbed his index finger against his thumb, a gesture that clearly referred to the money part of the deal, and then smiled and walked away.

Chet leaned forward with his elbows on his knees and looked down at his hands, as though preparing to read from a script.

"I'm a certified flight instructor, CFI, for single-engine, multi-engine, and instrument training. I went to a couple years of college in the School of Aeronautical Engineering at Cal Poly, the one in San Luis Obispo."

After a short pause, he continued.

"And my ultimate goal is to fly for the airlines someday. But for now, I'm buildin' flight time by giving instructions."

"How long have you been flying?" David asked.

Feeling a little more relaxed, Chet looked up from his hands and made eye contact with David.

"Since I was sixteen. I've got around twenty-five hundred hours total time. But don't get me wrong, I really like teaching. I just thought you ought to know about my airline goals."

David did need to know. He had learned to recognize God-given strengths in people and to build on those very strengths. There was a short pause and then Chet leaned back against the couch and put his feet on the beat-up coffee table strewn with outdated flying magazines. He was wearing cowboy boots and, from the look of them, it was not just a fashion statement.

"Now it's your turn. Why do you want to learn to fly?"

David collected his thoughts and, before answering the question, asked, "I kind of recognize that accent. I'm from Oklahoma. You?"

"No, Texas. I was raised about ten miles outside Odessa, out on the Permian Basin."

David smiled. "I was raised in Tulsa. I want to use flying in my business and see where it leads."

He resisted telling Chet about his relationship with God and how flying could be part of God's plan.

"OK, first thing is you need to get a flight physical. The names of a couple doctors are over there on the bulletin board. After you get it, call me and we'll set up your first lesson, your aircraft familiarization lesson."

As Chet spoke, he took his feet off the table and stood. His words and demeanor slowly changed from interviewee to flight instructor, and his six-foot-two-inch height added even more authority his words.

"Great, I'll get right on the physical and take care of the paperwork with the school. How do I pay you, direct or through the school?"

"Through the school. But you and me will work out the lesson schedule and flight times."

After a slight pause, Chet continued. "I'll work around your schedule, Dave, but I'm tied up Monday through Thursday nights. I've got another job to help with my income."

That statement piqued David's curiosity.

"Sure, no problem. I'm curious, what do you do?"

"Drive a truck. I run freight from San Diego to LA, reload, and haul back to San Diego. I'm usually back home by one or two in the morning."

David felt drawn to help this young man overcome the heavy work load and get on with his goal of flying.

"Wow, you're a hard-working guy. My schedule is nuts too, but I'm sure we can work something out that fits both of us. I'm good on weekends if that works for you."

Chet cracked a mischievous smile.

"Most weekends are OK, but I'm part of a rough stock rodeo team. We compete every few weeks or so, but other than that I'm good to go."

"And I thought I had a lot on my plate!" David exclaimed.

The two men walked to the parking lot together, shook hands, and, amid the pilot-inspiring sounds and sights of the airport, David promised to call Chet as soon as the flight physical was done.

As Chet drove away, David noticed the sticker on the bumper of his pickup truck: "Eight Seconds in the Arena Is Better Than a Lifetime in the Stands."

CHAPTER 16

The glazers were installing the last panel of full-height glass in the conference room wall, and the receptionist was loading a new black horizontal file when David walked in. She turned to greet him with a stack of manila folders on her lap and a toothy smile on her face.

"Good morning, Mr. Adams."

"Good morning, Jenny. Coffee ready?"

Jenny was David's first employee since his move from Tulsa to San Diego. Receptionist, bookkeeper, appointment secretary, file clerk, and, on most mornings, in charge of the coffee.

"Yes. And the briefcase you ordered is on your desk."

David raised an eyebrow and smiled.

"Excellent."

"Also, your eleven o'clock meeting is still on. Do you want to use the new conference room?"

David stepped into the conference room and did a quick visual inspection of the work in progress. The furniture was in place and the glass wall would be completed before the meeting, but the artwork was not hung and the deep gray paint of the display wall needed touching up.

In the short time he was away, Jenny had gotten his coffee and was standing beside her desk. Her dark brunette hair was pulled back in a bun, and the loose-fitting patterned dress did a good job of hiding the extra pounds she could not seem to lose. She held the steaming mug in both hands with the handle facing him.

He smiled as he reached for the coffee, "I'll have the meeting in my office."

He walked past the conference room and paused at the large open space next to his office. Two of the four AutoCAD drafting stations were up and running with young men he had hired through the New School of Architecture job placement program. The projects they were working on had been submitted for building permits and were in the final phase of corrections for resubmittal to the building departments.

After a glance back toward Jenny's desk, he stepped into his office and closed the door. Atop his desk was the new black leather hard-shell briefcase with tumbler security locks. It stood, handle up, on top of the blotter of his glass desktop, as if at attention. As he walked toward the desk, he admired the texture of the dark leather and gleam of the chrome and gold-trimmed hardware.

Gripping the handle, he picked it up and walked around the desk to his black leather executive chair. He sat down, set the briefcase on his lap, and pulled it open. Inside the case, he found the small tool used for setting the combinations of the tumblers. He opened the latches and set the combinations to the numbers he and Matt had agreed on: 666 on the left and 999 on the right.

CHAPTER 17

Weeks of training under Chet's teaching methods had put David in situations that could be best described as white-knuckled, physical and mental progressions that added more and more demands to each success. David understood that the rough-stock cowboy approach afforded the best flight instruction anyone could receive.

Chet was satisfied with David's ability to handle takeoff and landing emergency procedures and had moved to the next and equally important challenge: crosswind landings. He chose Brown Field in part because of the prevalent crosswind but also because the runways rest a mere one and a half miles from the Mexican border, adding more importance to David's place in sky.

David was overloaded, discouraged, and ready to quit. No matter how he approached the runway on final and no matter how he wished the airplane would track straight, he just couldn't keep the Piper Archer on the runway centerline. Every time the thing got its wheels on the ground. it headed for the gravel edge of the runway. Every time. And each time Chet had to rescue the rollout.

Finally, after demonstrating more patience than David was affording himself, Chet spoke up.

"OK, this time full stop and over to the ramp."

With mixed emotions of frustration and relief, David made the radio call required at uncontrolled airports.

"Brown Field traffic ... Archer One Three Juliet turning final Runway Two Six Right ... full stop ... Brown Field."

After a similar but marginally better landing, David taxied off the runway and stopped at the ramp. He turned slowly toward Chet and waited, unsure of what was coming but definitely sure of what he would say if he were in Chet's boots. With the engine at idle, Chet popped open the door to let some fresh air into the cockpit.

"Dave, you ever ride a horse?"

Caught completely off guard by a question that did not seem to relate to the circumstances, he looked past Chet and then slowly made eye contact with him.

"Uh, yeah. When I was a kid in Oklahoma."

"OK, did you ever ride a rental horse?"

David broke into a smile as the memories came.

"Oh, yeah. My dad would drive me out to Broken Arrow. A ranch there had horses to rent. We'd ride around the ponds and out into the hills.

"What do you remember most about the horses?"

"What I remember most was how they always tried to turn back. If you let them go, it was all over, but the shoutin' and saddle bouncin.' Like it or not you were going back to the barn."

Chet nodded his head and smiled.

"Well, Dave, whether it's an airplane or a horse ..."

His facial expression transformed into a look of profound seriousness and he continued.

"You got to be in charge of where it goes and what it does. Airplanes can seem to have a mind of their own. They don't. So if you lose it, you take it back. Don't let the thing make your decisions for you.

And on short final with a wind like this, you've got to cross control the airplane all the way to the ground with the nose pointing straight down the centerline. You've done it before. This is just a stiffer crosswind."

As the rental horse imagery soaked in, Chet unlatched his seatbelt and stepped out onto the wing.

"Dave, you can do this. We both know you can. Now I'm gonna wait out here and watch, just like we did when you first soloed. You get up there and do three touch-and-goes on centerline. Then taxi over here and get me. Remember, you can do anything you put your mind to. I've got my handheld receiver and I'll be listening."

Then he closed the door, stepped off the wing, and gave a thumbs-up signal as he walked away from the airplane.

David knew Chet was right, and the power of that knowledge filling him began to dissolve his frustration.

"Brown Field ... Archer One Three Juliet taking Runway Two Six Right ... touch-and-go ... Brown Field."

Flying without Chet in the cockpit ready to save the day and keep him from drifting into Mexico sharpened his resolve to meet the challenge. All three approaches were good and each time the little Archer tried to drift left, off centerline, David was more aggressive with right rudder and left aileron. Just like pulling the reigns harder until the thing finally submitted. After the last landing, David taxied over to the grassy area where Chet was standing picking his teeth with a blade of grass. He flicked it into the wind and climbed into the cockpit.

"Good job. Let's go home, I've got a date."

Being the first time that Chet had mentioned his social life, David could not resist probing a little.

"A date? Anyone special?"

"Nope. Just a gal I met at the rodeo. How about you? Got a girlfriend?"

David was sorry he had broached the subject.

"No. Married, divorced, and too busy to get involved. Let's go home."

CHAPTER 18

Three weeks following the crosswind landing practice, David was flying the same little Piper Archer solo, but this time with his FAA check ride behind him, his brand new pilot's certificate in his pocket, and Chet waiting for him at the airport.

It was not all that hard. He knew what to do and he did it—emergency procedures, stalls, steep turns. turns on a point, and landings. All familiar and all done pretty well. And on occasion, even though Chet was not in the airplane with him, David could hear his voice.

Remember, you can do anything you put your mind to.

Chet was leaning against the Coke machine with a Dr. Pepper in his hand, watching, when David landed and taxied up to the flight school fuel pumps. David shut down the engine, climbed out of the airplane, and walked toward Chet.

When he was within earshot, Chet called out, "You a pilot or not?"

"Yup," David responded with a grin plastered across his face.

"I knew you could do it."

Then the smiling expression of Chet's face slowly turned somber.

"Dave, there is something I need to talk to you about." He turned toward the café door.

"Come on in. I'll buy you a pop."

He walked into the café ahead of David and sat in a booth away from the people sitting along the counter seats. David slid onto the slick plastic booth across the table.

"What's up? Everything all right?"

Chet looked past him for a few seconds and then made eye contact.

"Well, yeah, everything is all right, except I can't take you up on that corporate pilot job you offered. I've finally got a chance to fly commercial."

"What airline?" David asked, now focused on Chet's success instead of his own.

With a smile and a sigh of relief, Chet answered. "Continental. Commuters at first, probably propjets."

Then he leaned forward and continued.

"I've got a guy I want you to meet. I've known him about three years. He works for the FAA, but now he's looking for a job where he can fly. He's got a Piper Seneca over at Montgomery Field and sometimes I use it for twin engine training. I'm bettin' he's got everything you need to be your corporate pilot. And I trust him. Let me get you two together and if you like him, I'll stick around long enough to help you and him find the right airplane for your mission. Deal?"

At first, David did not respond as he processed the new turn of events. Then after what felt to Chet like a silent form of hell, he finally answered. "Deal. When can I meet him?"

During the painful pause in the conversation, Chet realized that in the rapid fire unloading of information, he forgot to tell David the name of his possible replacement.

"His name is Tom, Tom Winslow. I'll have him call you."

As they walked out of the café toward the parking lot, David said, "I'm going to miss you, Chet. And there are a lot of things I wanted to tell you. Things about God, Jesus, and my life with Him."

Chet stopped and turned toward David.

"I can tell there's somethin' goin' on with you and God, Dave. Like all those days that were forecast to be bad that always seemed to clear up when you scheduled a lesson. Stuff like that. But Dave, honestly, if there really is a loving God, well if there is, why do bad things happen to good people? That really hangs me up."

Before David could respond, Chet suddenly changed the subject. "I've been doin' some research on twins, and there are some good deals on Cessna 414s and 421s. Want me to start looking for you?"

Seeing Chet's discomfort and hearing his quick move to change the subject, David allowed the conversation to fall back to earth.

"You bet. I'm doing enough out-of-state work to justify it. Have your friend call me and get me the info on the Cessnas."

They drove away from the airport, each toward separate goals and each carrying the strange emotional weight that comes upon people when sad changes birth new beginnings.

CHAPTER 19

"See you tonight!" Tom shouted out the window as he backed the six-year-old Chevy Tahoe out of the garage.

Margie smiled and waved back after setting the laundry basket on top of the washing machine.

"Good luck. Love you!"

As the garage door slowly rolled down, he nodded toward the tarp-covered Corvette sitting on blocks in the garage.

Maybe this job will give me the time and money to get you running again. If Chet's right, this is the offer of the century. It better be since Mac screwed me out of the examiners spot, the bastard.

The traffic grew heavier as he neared David Adams's office complex, and his thoughts turned to the interview.

I like the guy. I hope he's real. Getting a second interview, that's a good thing. The money and benefits are good, but I'll be away from home a lot. God, I hate interviews.

He parked near the building and walked the short distance to the lobby. Unaware of the divine guidance sculpting his professional and spiritual future, he rode the elevator alone, grateful for a last chance to shake off the interview jitters.

"Good morning, Mr. Winslow. I'll tell Mr. Adams you're here."

"Thanks," he said as he selected one of the three black leather lobby chairs, the one with its back to the wall. The symbolism escaped him.

He was barely seated when he saw David Adams walking toward him past the conference room. Quickly standing back up, he made eye contact with him and waited for a response.

"Great to see you again, Tom." David said and then nodded toward the conference room.

"Let's go in here where we can talk in relative privacy."

Tom took a seat at the conference table directly across from the small pile of papers and photographs David had placed there in anticipation of their meeting. Then after advising Jenny to hold his calls, David closed the door and sat down across the table from Tom.

"The references you gave me all had excellent things to say about you and your flying background. But honestly, the one that carries the most weight is Chet. He feels really good about you stepping in for him."

"Thanks," Tom said with a slightly nervous edge on his voice. "Chet's a good guy."

David slid the small stack of photographs and specification sheets toward him.

"He tells me the two of you have reduced the selection down to these three. True?"

Tom looked at the photographs and broke into a confident smile.

"Yes, that's true. But I think we should start with the 421. It's the exact same airframe as the 414s but with bigger engines, better performance, and more useful load."

He slipped one of the photographs from the stack and tapped its glossy surface.

"This one is right here in San Diego."

David leaned back in his chair and, after a short pause, changed the subject slightly.

"OK, Tom. But let's get you on the payroll before we take this any further. Are the salary and benefits we talked about good enough for now?"

"Uh, OK. Yeah, good. I'm, uh, I'm ready to start." The words struggled to get past his surprise at the sudden good news.

David stood and Tom quickly followed, offering a handshake.

David grasped his hand firmly and asked the next question that finished opening the new door to the future.

"How soon can you get us a ride in that 421?"

"Probably tomorrow. I'll get on it and call you this afternoon. Do you want me to call Chet too?"

"Yeah, great idea. Work it out and let me know."

Tom headed for the door to the elevator and then, just before David disappeared into his office, Tom got his attention.

"See you tomorrow, boss!"

CHAPTER 20

"November Five Three Seven Eight Mike. Can't miss it. It's the biggest twin on the ramp. Chet's already looking it over, and I'm starting on the log books. See you when you get here."

The message was from Tom. He had called when David was driving through the cell phone dead zone that seemed to surround Grossmont Hospital and the section of freeway that went by it. But that was when traffic was moving. Now he was parked in the number two lane of eastbound Interstate 8, trapped in a two-mile-long backup of impatient motorists and truckers. He tapped the rim of the steering wheel and pondered the changes that seemed to be just around the corner and inevitable.

The size and complexity of a Cessna 421 seemed overwhelming when compared to the simplicity of the Piper Archers and Tom's twin engine Piper Seneca. There is no doubt that this was a huge step. An airplane this complex needs a full-time corporate pilot, not just to fly, but to keep track of maintenance, operational costs, and trip planning. And the ...

Brrrraaaaapppp.

David's introspection was suddenly interrupted by the blast of an air horn behind him. The traffic was beginning to move and David was not. He waved an apology to the impatient trucker and quickly accelerated way from the growling big rig. Within a quarter of a mile, he took the Main Street exit, turned onto Bradley, and, after a few blocks, arrived at the security gate to the airport parking ramp. After referring to the yellow Post-It stuck to the dashboard, he punched the code number into gate's keypad. It slowly rolled open, and David scanned the rows of airplanes looking for "the biggest twin on the ramp."

Tom saw him at the gate and made a cell phone call to guide him in.

"Dave, look over to your right."

David pulled forward enough for the gate to roll closed behind him and looked down the last row of small airplanes where Tom was holding his hand in the air and waving. Another person whom David did not recognize was standing near Tom.

"Gotcha," David said and began cautiously driving past the first row of small airplanes. Some of them were polished and brightly colored, but others looked forgotten except for the birds that seemed at home on the vertical stabilizers. Ahead, at the end of the row, he saw the big white twin with Tom standing next to the tall rudder and tail. He parked near Tom.

"What a great looking airplane."

"Yeah, so far it looks pretty good," Tom responded as he opened the driver's door. "Dave, this is Mark. He's the broker."

David returned the broker's handshake and smiled.

"Too bad you heard me say that. The price probably just went up."

The broker smiled back.

"No. It is what it is. I'll stay out of the way while you guys do your thing."

With that, he walked to his car and busied himself in paperwork and cell phone calls.

"N5378M" was painted in twelve-inch-high black print across both sides of the vertical stabilizer and rudder, just below a slightly faded six-inch-tall decal of the American flag. In aviation language, all letters are spoken as words, for example, A is Alpha, B is Bravo, C is Charlie, and on and on. Therefore, using pilot language, this big twin was called November Five Three Seven Eight Mike.

It stood tall on beefy tricycle landing gear, slightly nose high and looked poised to go. Most twin engine airplanes have wings with engines, but this thing had engines with wings. The massive, streamlined, louvered engine cowlings bulged like aluminum muscles, each hulking behind big three-bladed propellers. Out on the tip of the wings were long, streamlined fuel tanks, resembling finless sharks, each with a nose and tail extending beyond the leading and trailing edges of the wings.

Everyone, pilots and passengers, enters through a clamshell door on the side of the fuselage just behind the left wing. When the two-piece door opened, the lower portion swung down, providing three built-in steps up into the cabin. From there, passengers walked forward, a little stooped, past the executive seats to a narrow opening in the forward bulkhead that separated the cockpit from the cabin. With that setup, David could fly with Tom and then move back to the cabin and read, work, or sleep when the mood struck him.

After a slow and introspective walk around the airplane, David climbed into the cabin and sat in one of the four gray leather seats. They showed some faint cracks and wear, as leather does, but still had a few years of life remaining. The seats faced each other in pairs, and the arrangement allowed a small table to be extracted from the cabin wall, separating the seats much like a small desk with chairs on each side.

Tom finished his review of the log books, climbed into the cabin, and sat across the aisle from David.

"The logs look good, and I didn't find any damage history. Let me get up there with Chet and see what the panel looks like."

He climbed forward to join Chet in the cockpit, and David stowed the small table in its vertical slot along the fuselage wall.

Now, with room to stretch his legs, he rested his feet on the opposite seat and felt the lingering nervousness slowly slip away. He put his hands behind his head in a stretching motion and watched Tom and Chet discussing the instrument panel.

This just might be the perfect airplane for me.

That thought floated around in David's mind like a ride on a carousel with a prize when you catch the ring.

Tom looked back from the pilot's seat.

"OK, boss, we're ready to take her up. Chet and I think it would be better if you stayed on the ground. You all right with that?"

"Sure. You guys go ahead. Good flight."

He climbed down the stair door, and Tom pulled it closed behind him. Then, moving to a position a few yards away from the left wingtip, he watched Tom climb into the pilot's seat and talk to Chet in the co-pilot seat beyond David's view.

Tom turned toward the small open storm window next to the pilot's seat and shouted.

"Clear left!"

The big three-bladed propeller started turning, and the left engine fired up. A deep, throaty roar filled the air and shook the ground under David's feet, slowly changing to a heavy rumbling as the engine settled into idle. Then, over the sound of the running engine, he heard the right engine come to life. A phrase that captured the hearty masculine sounds popped into David's mind.

Whoa … audible testosterone!

The novelty of that thought actually caused him to glance under the beast almost expecting to see a pair of steel spheres suspended below the rear of the fuselage. In the excitement of the moment, David spoke out loud, barely hearing himself over the heavy rumbling of the big engines.

"Pilots call their airplanes 'she' but not this bad boy. This is definitely 'he.'"

Tom gave David a thumbs–up signal, waved, and then released the brakes. The engines responded as he pushed the throttles slightly forward. The big airplane rolled with surprising ease and turned away, enveloping David in the windblast of the propellers and the rumble of the engines. In anticipation of the future, he verbally christened the newly found aluminum prize.

"Five Three Seven Eight Mike. Big Mike. Yup, Big Mike."

David's cell phone rang, the screen indicating that the office was calling. He turned his back to the departing wind and answered.

"David here. What's up?"

Jenny's normally calm voice had an excited ring to it as she asked for his advice. "Mr. Adams, what should I do with the checks that came in today?"

"Just deposit them as usual. Why?"

Her answer was a mixture of words and giggles. "Well, sir … well, it will be a rather large deposit. Checks arrived from three separate clients, and it all comes to $482,000.37."

A smirk like grin glowed on David's face as he answered.

"Oh, that."

"You must have made some collection calls. Well, it certainly worked."

David remembered the spiritual stand he had taken, and knowing that the only call he had made was a faith-powered prayer, he responded to her assumption.

"Yeah, I did make a call. There will likely be more to come."

"Oh my God. More to come. That's wonderful, Mr. Adams. Will you be in the office later?"

David responded to her question, but his heart was already with Jesus and his eyes were on the sky above where *Big Mike* banked in a circling climb over the airport.

"No, I won't be in today. I'll see you tomorrow."

He felt like a little kid who has just been handed a present that was only hoped for. Flooded with an almost overwhelming rush of emotions, he turned off the cell phone, walked back to his car, and leaned against the driver's door. With his face turned up toward the heavens, he confessed his surprise.

Father, Father, Father. Thank you. My God, my Wonderful God, thank You. Please show me, guide me. I want to use this wisely. Please show me. Thank you Father.

God's short and powerful response immediately filled David's mind and heart.

Prove Me.

The intimacy of the holy communication caused everything around him to fade away—the airport, the hangars, the sounds of cars, airplanes, and people. Everything. And in that otherworldly place, alone with Jesus, David answered.

"Lord, I know that buying this airplane is the right thing to do. I know that hiring Tom was the right thing to do. Father, thank You. I'll give ten percent of all that comes in to the people that You guide me to."

As the earthly sounds around him began to grow louder and louder, God whispered a loving challenge in words that filled him with emotional warmth and security.

Yes, David. Prove Me.

God had used those encouraging yet challenging words many times with David, prompting him and Matt to dig into the Scriptures and pray for wisdom to understand, as much as people can, what it means to "prove God." Matt had approached the answer with an eye toward mathematics and David with the tools of architectural engineering. They both agreed that the term "to prove" in math and engineering simply meant to confirm, by proven facts, that a thing is real or trustworthy, like calculating parts of a structure to prove that it will carry the intended load, without failing.

But it was through Scripture that God gave them the answer. Matt had used the "Scripture search" feature on his laptop to discover it: "Now faith is the substance of things hoped for, the evidence of things not seen."

Although Matt had found other Scriptures that helped them understand what it meant to prove God, it was that Scripture, Hebrews 11:1, that opened their minds. It is faith, not calculations or manmade work, that proved God. It is not to prove oneself worthy to God, but rather to prove that God is worthy by trusting Him completely, allowing Him to demonstrate His power and presence in everything and to believe with such confidence in Him that invisible becomes visible. Hope becomes reality.

The familiar rumble of Big Mike's engines caught David's attention as his thoughts returned to earth. He turned in the direction of the sound and saw Chet giving a thumbs-up through the co-pilot's window as the big twin gently slowed to a stop. David continued to watch as Tom completed the shutdown procedures and Chet opened the cabin door.

Chet shouted toward David and stepped out of the airplane. "Well, she looks pretty good."

Then he ambled up to David and held out his hand. "I guess this is it. Tom's got you now, and I feel real good about that."

Caught off guard by the suddenness of Chet's departure, David quickly responded.

"Chet, are you sure about this? Are you definitely in with the airline, because if you're not we can work something out here?"

Chet looked away for a moment.

"No, everything is 'go' with Continental. The money will be tight for a while, but everything is go."

David sensed there was more he could do for Chet. He reached out his hands and placed them on Chet's shoulders, a symbolic gesture that said, "Please don't go yet."

"Can you come by the office tomorrow? I'd like to know more about that."

"Sure, I can come by in the morning. That OK?"

"How's nine o'clock?"

"That's good for me."

Chet turned to shake hands with Tom, who had just walked up beside David.

"See you, Tom. Take good care of yourself. I'll try to stay in touch." Chet told him.

For a moment, all three men stood together in the shadow of Big Mike and found themselves unable to leave, held there by the bond that God was creating in them.

Then the broker walked up to the group.

"What do you think?"

David saw Tom nodding in approval and then looked at Chet, who gave him another thumbs-up, this one from the waist.

"I think you need to sell me that airplane. Let's talk money."

With that, the men went their separate ways: David and the broker to work out the deal, Tom to rush home and tell Margie the good news, and Chet to start packing.

CHAPTER 21

Tom called Margie from the car on the way home, and she was waiting at the front door as he pulled into the driveway.

"Well, Mr. Corporate Pilot, welcome home."

He embraced her on the front door stoop and briefly enjoyed the scent of her hair and mildly perfumed neck. Then he whispered, "We did it, Margie. We did it. This is what I've been waiting for. We did it."

She returned his embrace with a gentle hug and then held his face in her hands and kissed him.

"Come inside and tell me all about it."

They curled up on the big sectional couch, and Tom placed her left hand between the palms of his hands and squeezed. Then, before he began, he paused to admire her youthful beauty, preserved behind the blue eyes that still held him captive. Her dark brunette hair was pulled back into a shoulder-length ponytail, and her petite figure was hidden inside baggy gray sweat pants and one of Tom's white T-shirts, her typical housecleaning uniform. Her bare feet were curled up beneath her on the couch as she waited for Tom to speak.

"First things first. Thanks for putting up with me and my griping about the FAA and my family and my fear of having kids."

She smiled as Tom continued, rambling like a little kid telling about his first day of school.

"David and his company are really great people. The pay's good. We'll have medical insurance that includes dental, maternity, and we found a really cool airplane. It's not new, but I really like it. David's going to pay for me to go to SimCom every year to fly their simulator. And I'm in charge of trip planning, scheduling all the maintenance. There are annual office retreats, and all the people are really great."

Margie, although listening intently, was processing Tom's remarks about kids and maternity insurance.

"Tommy," she interrupted and placed her right hand on his knee, squeezing gently in a pulsing rhythm. "Does this mean we can have a baby now?"

A little surprised by the question, Tom smiled softly and looked deeply into her eyes. There he saw the familiar come hither look and sparkle that she projected like a light into his soul.

"Let's do."

Without speaking, Margie stood, held her hands out toward Tom, and nodded her head toward the bedroom.

He smiled one of those half smiles, mimicking Harrison Ford's Hollywood trademark, and reached up as if to take her hands into his. Then, suddenly, he grabbed her by the waist and pulled her onto his lap. He had not felt that mischievous since their honeymoon in Hawaii, which was also the last time he felt good about their future.

Margie squealed, put both hands on his chest and pushed back, mimicking the vigor that pulled her down.

"Tommy!" she giggled. "Not here."

"OK," he responded, as he stood and scooped her up into his arms.

Securely cradled in his arms, she clung to his neck and laid her head against his shoulder as she drifted past the front door, where Tom flipped the deadbolt to lock.

Sensual, emotional, and spiritual nonverbal communication, unique to a husband and wife, flowed between them as he gently lowered her down on their pillow-laden bed. There was nothing in their world but the two of them, entwined in passion, love, and honeymoon lust.

CHAPTER 22

Jenny's voice interrupted the silence as she approached his desk. "Mr. Adams, excuse me. The mail just arrived, and there are more checks."

David looked up and smiled. "Thanks. Just deposit them for now. I'm still waiting for some guidance on that."

She assumed he meant a call from Matthew Solman. "Mr. Rawlins is here. I put him in the conference room, if that's all right."

"Great. Tell him I'll be right there. And could you close my door?"

She promptly left the room and closed the door as instructed. Sitting alone in his office, David asked God for one last assurance that what he was about to do was the right thing.

"Lord, I believe Chet is one of those who can benefit from the money. It's your money, and I only want to be the delivery boy. I believe that the urgency I feel to help him is from you."

This time, instead of words, God answered by increasing David's feelings of urgency and the correctness of the decision. Recognizing the answer to prayer and knowing that Chet was waiting, David grabbed his checkbook and wrote a check for twenty thousand dollars. He slipped it into his shirt pocket and headed for the conference room.

"Chet! Sorry to make you wait."

"No problem, Dave. Your girl got me some coffee and a bagel."

David sat at the head of the table and signaled to Jenny for a cup of coffee for himself.

"Chet, I'm going to miss you, but I'm really happy for you. I know this is your dream."

Chet leaned forward and looked down at the palms of his hand, much like he did when he first met David at the flight school.

"Yeah, it really is."

Then he looked up at David and continued."I really didn't know how much that truck driving gig was holding me back 'til you convinced me to quit and focus on flying. I'll never forget you sayin' that I was being held back by an eighteen wheeler chained to my foot."

Driven as he was to act on God's instructions, David jumped right to the subject.

"Chet, tell me about your training at Continental. You know, how long you'll be in training and how good is the money."

Jenny interrupted briefly to bring David's coffee as Chet leaned back in his chair, holding his coffee cup in both hands.

"The training isn't bad. I'll be in Chicago at the company school for a couple months, then simulator training. After that, I'll fly 'right seat' for I don't know how long. The money will work out. It's tight, but it'll work out. My momma says she might help some."

Then in an attempt to change the subject, Chet said, "Did I tell you she's moving to a retirement home near Palm Springs?"

Cautiously, David leaned forward and looked him squarely in the eyes.

"Chet, I want to help you with the money. Can you tell me more about how much you need? Say for the next twelve months. And how much you'll get from Continental."

Chet understood David's intent but to him handouts and charity felt insulting and humiliating. And although he did his best to control the tone of his response, the words carried with them the sting of offense.

"You know, Dave, I really appreciate it, but I really don't need your help."

"I know, Chet. But the money isn't mine to give. It's just passing through my account and into yours. So tell me, in a perfect world, how short are you?"

Partially because of guilt from the tone of his response and with a growing curiosity of whose money David was talking about Chet answered.

"A lot. I figure about ten thousand. Continental only pays fifteen thousand for the first year. But it'll all work out."

David laughed out loud and slapped a hand on the conference table, almost spilling his coffee.

"Yes, it will!"

Not sure of David's outburst, Chet sat back in his chair and waited for him to explain.

"I'm sorry, Chet, but God has such an amazing sense of humor. I've been entrusted with some money to pass on. He put you on my heart, and I already had a figure in my head before our meeting. My problem, it turns out, isn't how much to give you. My problem is to convince you to accept it."

As he listened, Chet's mind flooded with questions flowing from his injured spirit.

God? Money for me? I know he's into God, but money for me? How does God figure into that?

David continued. "Chet, do you remember me telling you that Jesus is like the 'Hound of Heaven.' He tracked me until I found him? Do you remember that?"

Chet answered cautiously. "Yeah, Hound of Heaven. I remember."

David pulled the prewritten check from his shirt pocket. "Well, my friend, Jesus is tracking you down."

He handed Chet the gift and continued. "Here is twenty thousand dollars. It's not mine, it's yours. Expect great things my friend."

Chet sat holding the check, staring at it, speechless. Then, after a few seconds, when he felt somewhat recovered, he tried to speak but could not. The tough young cowboy wanted to look up at David, but his eyes were tearing and short sobs prevented him from speaking.

Seeing his helplessness, David stood, walked around behind him, and placed his hands on Chet's shoulders.

"God loves you Chet. He really loves you. I'll go to my office and leave you alone with Him for a while."

David quietly left the conference room, closed the door, and, after instructing Jenny not to disturb him, slipped into the prayerful sanctuary of his office. His desk had been a prayer platform many times before, and now again he sat holding his head in his hands and praying.

"Father, thank You. Be with Chet, draw him close to You."

A few minutes later, David returned to the conference room, but Chet was gone and on the table lay a note scribbled on a steno pad.

Dave, thank you. I will use it wisely. Thanks again. I'll call once in a while. Chet.

Confused and a little saddened, David walked past Jenny's desk.

"I'm going to call it a day. Hold my calls."

He rode the elevator down and walked toward his car, worried, doubting his actions, and feeling that somehow he had failed.

I must have been too pushy, too cocky. God I hope not.

Suddenly his cell phone rang, the screen indicating that Tom was calling.

"Hi, Tom, what's up?"

"Dave, I'm glad I caught you. The office said you had left. Here ... my wife wants to talk to you."

"Hello, Mr. Adams? This is Margie, Tom's wife."

"Yes, hi. I look forward to meeting you."

"Well, I want to thank you. Tommy is so happy. I just wanted to thank you. We would like to have you over for dinner sometime."

The joy and sincerity in her voice began to wash away the worry and doubt that hung on David's emotions.

"Sure, that would be great. Tom can get my schedule from the office and we'll get together. Thank you. I'm real glad to have Tom on board, so I guess we're all happy."

"Well, good-bye. I look forward to meeting you."

"Me too. Good-bye."

Grateful for the cleansing effect the call had on his emotional funk, David prayed.

OK, Lord. Thank You. I needed that.

He turned around and headed back to the office, where Jenny greeted him with news he needed to hear. "Oh, Mr. Adams ... good. Mr. Rawlins called just after you left. I asked him to leave a message on your voice mail."

A mixture of relief and worry spun through David's mind. He quickly shut himself in his office, dialed up his messages, and found Chet's.

"Dave. This is Chet. Sorry I had to take off so quick. I got a call from Continental. They said I can get a ride to Chicago in the jump seat of a 747 leaving LA tomorrow morning. I had to run to the bank and finish packing. Someday, someway, I will find a way to pay you back."

His voice began to tremble as he struggled to continue.

"Thank you, David. You are a real friend. See you. Bye."

At peace with his world and feeling confident that he had done the right thing, David leaned back in his office chair, put his feet up on the desk, and spoke aloud to the empty room.

"Airplane, corporate pilot. Now, Lord, let's see where this goes."

Just then Jenny's voice came over the intercom. "Mr. Adams, the contractor for the Tucson project is on line one."

David picked up the receiver, leaned back in his black leather office chair, and took a deep breath. If the players were in place, it would work. "David Adams here."

Although the call came from inside the construction trailer, background sounds of nail guns, skip loaders, backhoes, and shouting men caused the contractor to raise his voice over the muffled din.

"Hello, David. I've got the concrete sub here with me, and he's got some questions about the new rebar layout that showed up on the drawings we got yesterday."

"But first I need to know if he agreed to work nights and meet the scope of work requirements we talked about."

"Yeah, he did."

"How close is he to the estimate?"

"He needs the work, so no problem. But he needs to talk to you personally."

"Put him on."

There was a pause and the receiver banged against the desk as the contractor passed the phone to the subcontractor.

"Mr. Adams?"

"Yes."

"Oh, hello. My name's Cliff, and like he said, I got some questions."

"Go ahead."

"Well, sir, these are pretty big changes. I guess I need to know if you're gonna help if I have trouble with the building inspector and such."

"Absolutely, Cliff. Are you aware that I got your name from your pastor?"

"Yeah, he told me, and I really appreciate it."

"Cliff." David paused and took a deep breath. "There are specific reasons I'm hiring you. I will fly out next week and we can talk about it. Meanwhile, lay out all the perimeter steel and forms except the area that's clouded on the drawings as Revision 14. Any questions for now?"

"No. I guess I'll see you sometime next week."

"All right then. See you next week."

David gently placed the receiver down and closed his eyes.

Lord, thank You for bringing me this man. Now please lead me on. I am ready and I am Yours.

Then he pressed the telephone intercom button. "Jenny."

"Yes, sir."

"Have Tom look at the weather for a trip to Tucson next week."

"Do you care which day?"

"The sooner, the better."

CHAPTER 23

In the predawn darkness, David backed out of his driveway for the short trip to the airport. He crested the hill on Fletcher Parkway and was greeted by the faint pink glow on the horizon beyond the still-sleeping city of El Cajon. Sunrise would come soon.

After driving a few more miles through the empty streets, he arrived at Gillespie Field and pulled up to the gate near the hangar. He keyed in the security code and waited for the notoriously slow gate to open. While he waited, he could see the silhouette of Big Mike parked on the ramp ahead and the movement of a flashlight beam under the left wing.

As he watched the end of the gate finally roll through the beam of his right headlight and continue into the darkness, he asked for help.

Lord, give me wisdom and protection for this trip. And thank You for Tom.

His silver Mercedes C430 sedan glided smoothly over the gate's steel-track threshold and pulled up to Big Mike's left wing. Tom walked toward the car, flashlight in hand.

"Good morning, Tom."

"Morning, Dave. Preflight's done except for bleeding the tanks."

Tom always drained a few ounces of fuel out of each tank before the first flight of the day and again after refueling since a little condensation commonly developed inside the fuel tanks, especially on cool days. If left to accumulate, it could get into the fuel lines and cause an engine failure.

Tom continued. "I'll load your stuff into the nose compartment and then you can park while I finish up out here."

While Tom transferred the suitcases and briefcase from the car to the airplane, David looked east and saw the jagged outline of El Capitan and the Cuyamaca Mountains as the intensifying pink glow of the sunrise quietly announced the calm morning. He chuckled to himself.

It's quiet now, but just wait until Big Mike fires up!

After parking the car, David walked the short distance back to Big Mike and called out to Tom.

"I'll sit in the back this leg. I've got some reading to do before today's meetings."

Tom shouted back from under the right wing.

"Coffee's in there. Climb in. I'll get the door and chocks. Car locked?"

David answered over his shoulder as he ascended the stairs into the dimly lit cabin.

"Yup, good to go."

Tom completed the preflight inspection, climbed aboard, and closed the cabin door. He stopped at David's seat on the way to the cockpit.

"The weather looks good. Should be a smooth ride."

Then he continued forward, slid into the pilot's seat, and David settled into his favorite cabin seat. It faced forward and was located just behind the right wing. From there, he could see Tom's side of the instrument panel, and the view outside was far enough aft to see the ground below.

Tom fired up the engines and David chuckled aloud.

"Good morning, El Cajon!"

Of course, Tom could not hear him with his headset on and the engines rumbling.

The control tower was not in operation and would not be for a couple hours. They taxied to the run-up area where Tom did the pre-takeoff systems checks. When he was satisfied that everything was "go," he made the radio announcement required at uncontrolled airports.

"Gillespie Traffic ... Five Three Seven Eight Mike departing, Two Seven Right ... left downwind departure ... Gillespie Traffic."

He rolled onto the runway, stopped on the centerline, and pushed the throttles to full power. The roar of the engines at full power humorously reminded David of the "audible testosterone" description that popped into his head the day he bought Big Mike. They picked up speed straight down the centerline and lifted off for Tucson at 6:00 a.m, as planned.

The morning air was cool and calm, just what Big Mike liked for a good climb rate. With the nose pitched up, they roared into the sky at twelve hundred feet per minute. Then, at thirty-five hundred feet above the ground, Tom pulled the power back and trimmed for a five-hundred-feet-per-minute climb to their cruising altitude of thirteen thousand five hundred feet.

David whispered to himself, "Not bad for a thirty-five-year-old, seven-thousand-two-hundred-pound airplane with full fuel, baggage, and two on board."

The ride at cruise altitude was smooth and cloudless, just as Tom predicted, allowing David to enjoy a cup of coffee and study the project files with his feet propped up and his seat reclined.

This is the way to travel. Thank you, Lord.

Then, as he tried to read, the steady drone of Big Mike's engines slowly lulled him to sleep. Comfortable, warm, and grateful.

After what seemed like only a few minutes to David, he was awakened by a change in the sounds as Tom began stage cooling the engines for descent. Reducing the power in small increments helps the engines and turbo chargers cool slowly instead of being shock cooled by the cold air at altitude. So far the technique had kept the engines healthy.

David secured his briefcase with a seatbelt and climbed forward to join Tom for the approach and landing.

He settled into the co-pilot's seat, snapped on the seatbelt, and slipped on his headset, the same headset he used during his hours of training with Chet.

"What's up? How do we look?"

"The winds are light and from the east. We'll probably get Two Niner Right."

As they made the descent into Tucson airspace, approach control handed them off to the tower. Tom switched to the new frequency. Pilots and air traffic controllers refer to altitudes by a specific number sequence to avoid verbal confusion that could result in midair collisions. For example, one one thousand is 11,000 feet, and one one thousand five hundred is 11,500 feet. "Tucson control … Five Three Seven Eight Mike … one one thousand five hundred with information Bravo."

"Seven Eight Mike … Tucson … good morning … cleared to land runway Two-Niner Right … number three following a Learjet … report traffic in sight."

There were two private jets ahead and a twin Beechcraft on their tail as Big Mike merged into the conga line for Runway 29 Right. Out Tom's window, David could see a pair of military F18s on approach for the parallel runway.

Tom flared for a smoothed landing, got on the brakes hard, and took the first high-speed exit onto the taxiway.

David smiled.

"You greased it on, Tommy. Nice job."

CHAPTER 24

The ride from the airport to the construction site was slow as Tom guided the rental car through the Tucson morning commuter traffic that crept east on Interstate 10. As they approached Wilmot Road, he merged and took the exit.

Construction equipment and stacks of building materials could be seen ahead on the right as they neared Old Vail Connection Road. Tom slowly pulled off the pavement onto the graded dirt and drove toward the construction trailer. As he did, David studied the progress and was pleased to see that the perimeter forms around the underground parking garage were in place and men were tying off the rebar. Tom slowed to a stop, and David climbed out with his briefcase in hand.

The contractor stepped out of the trailer and stood on the raised wooden platform that served as stairs and landing. He pointed toward the northeast corner of the project and shouted.

"Cliff's over there!"

David walked toward a group of men laying rebar in the forms. As he approached, one of them stood away from the group and raised his gloved hand.

"You Mr. Adams?"

"That's me. You Cliff?"

David stopped near a parked pickup truck, set his briefcase down on the left front fender, and signaled to Cliff.

"Come on over."

Cliff walked the short distance, wiping his forehead with an ungloved hand. His tanned face was smeared with a blend of sweat and dust that made his teeth seem too white to be his own.

"Good to meet you, Mr. Adams. I figure we got something in common if you know what I mean."

"Yes, Cliff, I believe we do, and you can call me Dave."

He looked at David with a small smile and a mischievous expression on his face.

"OK, Brother Dave."

"Brother Dave it is. But I prefer just Dave."

One of the men working on the rebar called out. "Cliff! When can we start on the last section?"

Before he could answer, David jumped in. "Come with me."

David grabbed his briefcase, and Cliff followed him to the unfinished section of work, the section clouded on the plans as Revision 14.

"Before you call your men over, I want to explain something to you."

Cliff held up his hand, signaling the men to keep working where they were.

"Cliff, can I count on you to follow my instructions?"

"Like I said on the phone, if you cover me, I'm OK with whatever you say."

David unlocked the latches of the briefcase, opened it, and pulled out a folded document. As he unfolded it, Cliff saw that it was a hand-drawn version of the same area as Revision 14.

"Good. Now, this is what I need you to do here and on the projects in Chandler and Goodyear. There won't be any steel in this area, and the slab will be two inches instead of six, creating a soft spot exactly thirty-two inches by thirty-two inches."

Cliff studied the sketch and rubbed his chin, trying to understand why this was necessary. But before he could speak,

David continued. "Place the original floor forms and steel, but don't tie it. Then, after the inspector signs off, relocate the steel as shown on this drawing and adjust the floor form to get the thinner section. Clear?"

"You know what could happen if we do that, don't you?"

"Yes, I do. And Cliff, there's more."

The growing secrecy caused Cliff to lean in closer, like a rookie in a huddle.

"I need you to do some welding."

"Sure. What on, the rebar?"

"No. There are garage air handlers coming and they need to be modified."

David pulled a letter-sized isometric drawing from his briefcase. "Each garage will have two air handlers. One is located as shown on the original drawings and the other, the one you will modify, goes over the soft spot."

David gave Cliff time to respond, but he only nodded and waited for more.

"OK. The drawing is self-explanatory, but I need you to be very clear on the hinged floor panel. It has to be exactly thirty-one and three-quarter inches square and swing freely on both directions, up and down."

Cliff picked up the isometric drawing and briefly studied the reinforcing angle iron and hinged panel design.

"Got it. And the panel goes over the soft spot, right?"

"Right. These drawings are for your eyes only. Burn them when you're done."

Then he took a cell phone from his briefcase and handed it to Cliff.

"Use this for calls to me—and only to me."

CHAPTER 25

The flight back from Tucson had been uneventful, and David was glad to be home because a partially completed project awaited him in his living room.

He sat on the living room floor dressed in gray sweats and running shoes, surrounded by tools, electrical parts, and a small heavy cardboard box. A stationary exercise bicycle stood nearby. He opened the box and pulled out an eighty-amp automobile alternator. The exercise bike had been modified with a pulley and belt attached to the drive wheel and a receiver for the alternator. And on the floor next to the bike was a four hundred-amp deep-cycle marine battery. If the prototype worked, it would be reproduced—twenty-eight times.

He scooted over to the bike and mounted the alternator onto the receiver. After connecting the wiring and amp gauge to the battery, he stood and stretched, raising his hands into the air.

"Let's see how this works."

With a white towel draped over his shoulders, he mounted the bike and began pedaling. The bike pedaled easily, and the alternator pulley spun freely. The ease of pedaling surprised him, and he switched on toggle mounted next to the amp gauge. Then his second surprise came: the alternator kicked in, the amp gauge sprang to life, and the pedals loaded down like lead weights. He struggled to maintain the pedaling speed until his legs felt like ice picks were stabbing his thighs.

"Ouch. We're gonna gear this down a couple notches."

The cell phone rang. Cliff's name flashed on the screen.

"Hello, Cliff."

"Hi, Dave. Just callin' to tell you the air handlers arrived. I'm gonna take half of 'em to my shop and start modifying. And the inspector signed off Tucson."

"Great. How are you handling the general contractors?"

"They think I'm fixin' ductwork in the air handlers, and I'll make the rebar changes overnight before the pour."

"Any questions about the modifications to the air handlers?"

"No, I get it. They should be ready in a couple days. I'm markin' 'em with a weld on the corners so we can tell 'em apart from the other ones."

"Don't make it too obvious."

"It's a small cross. Just seemed right to me."

CIRCA AD 2007

CHAPTER 26

There was no response.

David picked up the handset and canceled the call to Tom. The long hours had slowed his stride, and he was beginning to look his age. The youthful sparkle of his eyes was still there but now tempered with a depth of spiritual growth and maturity, giving proof to the saying that a man's eyes are the windows to his soul.

His phone rang and he hit the speaker button. "This is David."

To his surprise, Chet's voice resounded inside the parked car. "Hi, Dave. We're on a weather layover in Atlanta, and I thought I'd check in. How are things out there?"

His confident, cheerful voice projected a clear picture of his successful career with Continental Airlines. David recognized the strong connection Chet had with him, almost like family. And he had grown accustomed to getting random calls from Chet every two or three months.

"Chet! How you doing?"

"Things are great."

"Here, too. Tom and I are getting a lot of use out of Big Mike, and business is good. What have you been up to?"

"Like I said, I'm on a layover in Atlanta. I may get the New York to Las Vegas run, don't know yet. If I do, maybe we can meet up there one day. I'll buy you dinner."

As happens with cell phones, and at the most inopportune times, the signal began to fail and David could only hear every third or fourth word.

"Chet, I'm losing you. Las Vegas sounds good. I'll try to get back to you. If you can hear me, see you later."

After waiting for a response and hearing none, he canceled the call and walked the short distance from his car to the office. The elevator ride up was sullen, and David dreaded the meeting. It was true that he was physically tired from the grueling work schedule, but it was the meeting with Tom that had him carrying an unfamiliar emotional weight.

Since joining the company, Tom had handled his responsibilities well: corporate pilot, trip planner, valet, weather watchdog, and more. But he had become pessimistic and overly cautious about flying, and pessimism was one of the few things David had little patience for. Until recently, it had only been a minor flaw in their relationship, but Tom's overly cautious trip planning had scrubbed several flights that David knew could have been made in Big Mike.

Margie and Tom had twins, a boy and a girl, and David was convinced that Tom's innately cautious nature had gotten worse since then. Often, almost as an admission of guilt, Tom reminded David how much he appreciated the company's respect and patience with his sometimes frustrating "no-go" recommendations. Both men knew of corporate pilots whose bosses insisted on flying regardless of weather conditions or potential problems with the airplane. They also knew those guys were rolling the dice.

David would not normally roll the dice or ask Tom to compromise, but this trip was different. He needed to go from San Diego to Phoenix and then on to Las Vegas and finally back to San Diego. Three states, three legs, two days. That trip, scheduled for the next day, was what the meeting was about and that was why David was sullen.

During an earlier trip-planning meeting, Tom had assured David that the leg to Phoenix would not be a problem. But he also warned that icing conditions and turbulence forecast between Phoenix and Las Vegas would probably prevent them from continuing on. If the forecast was correct, David would be flying commercial the rest of the way, and Tom would wait out the weather in Phoenix with Big Mike.

The staff had already gone home for the day when David walked toward the conference room where Tom was organizing the last few details of the trip, including getting online reservations with Southwest Airlines for David's Las Vegas leg. Determined to shake off the emotional funk, David burst into the room.

"Let's do this!"

Surprisingly unaffected by the sudden entrance and announcement, Tom calmly looked toward him.

"Alright, but we'll decide one leg at a time. Like I said yesterday, you may need to go commercial out of Phoenix. I've got you 'ticketless.'"

The pessimistic tone grated David's nerves. Tom was always the same when he felt conditions were not perfect for traveling in Big Mike. Pessimistic.

David sat his briefcase on the conference table and, although he appeared to be looking for something, he was actually buying time, trying to collect his thoughts and prepare a response.

"I know. What time do you want me at the airport?"

The building frustration was challenging his normal management style, and he knew that eye contact with Tom would reveal it. For several days, strong feelings about the trip had been growing within his mind and heart. Gut feelings. Feelings that hinted of something new coming into his life—possibly an opportunity to stretch his faith and prove his God.

This is not the time, and Tom is not the problem.

Those words passed through David's mind as he shook off the emotional weight.

Tom was packing charts into his flight bag and sensed David's stress.

"Five thirty; I'll have the coffee. Do you want bagels or anything?"

"No. Just the coffee and all three legs. No commercial unless we absolutely have to. Deal?"

Tom looked at David with a mischievous grin and answered in the tone of a person talking to a child.

"We'll see."

David cracked a smile that said, "There is more to this than you know," and challenged back.

"Yes … we'll see."

CHAPTER 27

After a textbook approach and landing, they taxied to the Cutter Aviation Terminal, where Tom parked Big Mike and unloaded the documents David needed for the day in Phoenix. They walked the short distance from the airplane to the terminal in uncharacteristic silence.

The temperature was warmer than normal for November, and the approaching cold fronts would lift the warm air, creating turbulence and a bumpy ride, probably with ice accumulation. Any visible moisture, rain, or clouds at or below zero degrees Celsius would freeze onto the airplane's propellers and leading edges of the wings and empennage. David did not ask Tom about the chances of going on to Las Vegas, and he suspected Tom did not want to tell him. He tossed his briefcase into the backseat of the rental car.

"I don't need you to drive me today. I would rather you stay at the airport, watch the weather updates, and get ready for our next leg to Las Vegas, hopefully tonight."

Tom nodded in agreement.

"OK, I'll see how the forecast looks. Don't forget, I've already got you ticketed on Southwest."

"I know. But we need to put more effort into getting there with Big Mike. Do what you can. I should be back by four thirty or five o'clock."

He drove away, hoping for a small miracle and with about that much faith. The meeting at the Las Vegas warehouse the next morning was essential. The crates were packed with almost everything needed for the final phase of the projects. David had to be there and without a paper trail, like an airline ticket.

By 4:45 p.m. David had finished meeting with the night crew of the Goodyear project. He started the drive back to the airport and noticed the sky had changed to an ominous, solid overcast and a cold drizzle had begun to fall. In the distance, he could see the cloud bases resting on top of Superstition Mountain east of Phoenix. As he merged onto Interstate 10 West, he called Tom's cell phone hoping, but not really expecting, to hear good news about the night flight to Las Vegas.

"Tom, I'm done and heading your way. What do you think? Can we go tonight?"

David heard the familiar "unhappy weather watchdog" tone in Tom's voice as he apologetically answered. "Dave, the overcast has moved in, and the freezing levels are too low. I'm sorry, but we can't go tonight."

From inside the pilots' lounge, Tom was not aware that David was looking through the car's windshield directly at the problem as they spoke. He also could not see David holding his clenched fist in the air toward the overcast in symbolic rebellion.

"Tommy, I understand. But when I get back to the airport, show me the forecast for early in the morning. If we get out of here by five thirty, I can still get to the meeting."

Tom reluctantly agreed.

"Sure, but …"

Then realizing he had better not take it too far, he quickly corrected his response.

"Sure thing, I'll meet you in the Pilots' Lounge."

It took only twenty minutes for David to get back to Cutter, even with the heavy, late afternoon Phoenix traffic. He parked the rental car and found Tom in the pilots' lounge as planned.

"Show me what you've got," David said with as much optimism as he could muster.

Most of the general aviation pilots had scrubbed their flight plans due to the weather, and the pilots' lounge was vacant. They sat in swivel chairs in front of the weather computer, reading forecasts and studying the satellite and radar images on the monitor.

Tom spoke first.

"If there's going to be any improvement in the morning, it'll be marginal."

David did not respond but continued to study the images and text hoping to find a hole, a break, a window for them—something strong enough to convince Tom to "go for it." Tom never liked go for it when it came to trip planning, and David was not ready to give up. No, instead of quitting, David was ready to get serious about the situation and that included getting into some serious prayer. Not a foxhole prayer, but an "in His presence, Father and son, Daddy what can I do? I want Your will" kind of prayer.

Tom broke the silence.

"Dave, I've got us reservations at a nearby motel, and your Southwest flight isn't 'til six a.m. We'll have time to check the weather again in the morning before we decide. How about we get out of here?"

David agreed and they headed for the motel. While Tom drove, David used the time for introspection. His life had changed in style and perspective, no doubt. And there was no doubting that as he had grown closer to God, God had come closer to him. Just recently, David had read a Scripture in James, Chapter 4, promising that very thing. He also remembered someone saying, "If you don't feel close to God, ask yourself, 'Who moved?'"

David had learned that close to Him was where the answers were found. Close to Him was where the power awaited. Close to Him was where confusion, doubt, and the spirit of can't be done bit the dust.

CHAPTER 28

Tom's bed was hard, the towels were scratchy, the soap was too small, the room smelled like cigarettes, and the television remote was dead. He and David had a relatively silent dinner together, in part because of the long work day but also because neither wanted to talk about the Las Vegas leg.

He was lying on top of the bed covers, worrying. And as often happened with him, worry brought on insecurity and with it frustration, which grew into doubt of his judgment and skills. As he struggled with the seemingly insurmountable problem the weather had dumped on him, he confessed, "I'm pushing him too hard. He is the boss for God's sake. Seems like he's got more confidence in me than I've got in myself."

Then, in a snarling voice, "Damn remote doesn't work. Maybe the phone does."

He dialed his home telephone number and after obeying the necessary prompts for his credit card number, he heard Margie's sleepy voice. "Hello?"

"Hi, honey, hope I didn't wake you."

Her voice perked up a bit when she noticed the clock. "Are you OK? It's kind of late."

"Yeah, I'm OK. I just wanted to talk to you."

The tone of his voice betrayed his words, prompting her to challenge his white lie. "Something's wrong. What is it? Are you sick?"

"Well, no, I'm not sick. It's just that Dave and I are knocking heads about the trip to Vegas in the morning. He wants to go and I don't. He is the boss, for God's sake. Maybe I should just do what he says."

Accustomed as she was to dealing with his mood swings and self-imposed lack of confidence, she responded in a soft, almost motherly tone. "Honey, what you need is a good night's sleep. I'm sure that it will all work out in the morning. It's after midnight. Now go to sleep and call me tomorrow when it's all worked out. I love you."

Soothed by her voice and strengthened by her confidence, he answered. "You're right. Dave isn't going to push this too far. Besides, maybe the weather will open up like he says. Good night, honey.

One of the twins had awakened, and Margie climbed out of bed to take care of the noisy problem.

"I've got to check on the kids. Sleep tight, sweetheart."

She placed the telephone back on the nightstand.

Not realizing that she was gone, Tom went on to say, "Oh, and if anything ever did happen, don't let anyone have my log books. Burn them. Good night, honey."

He sat the handset back onto the telephone, unaware that she had not heard his instructions. The sound of the dial tone came on just as the handset met the cradle.

As he lay back, he remembered reading hundreds of accident reports, issued by the National Transportation Safety Board, when he worked for the FAA. The NTSB always included pilot error—always. It seemed that no matter how qualified the pilot, there was always something in the log books. Something to justify broad accusations that spawned insurance headaches and increased the pain for the pilot's loved ones.

He chuckled to himself as he remembered the pledge he made with Chet and two other pilots during an instructors meeting. It might have been Chet, he couldn't remember, but one of them determined that "burning the books" was the best way to battle the bureaucratic misuse of their personal records. They all agreed to spread the word, to stand united as pilots against the system. Tom's passive-aggressive side liked the idea.

CHAPTER 29

The terminal public address system was announcing the last call for Flight 66 to Las Vegas when Chet stuffed his overnight bag into the hanging locker next to the flight attendant's jump seat. The passengers in first class were being offered magazines and giving their drink orders. He stopped at the cockpit door and looked down the long aisle toward the aft section of the Boeing 757. A nearby flight attendant smiled and waved.

"Good afternoon, Captain Rawlins."

He smiled back warmly, slipped off his cap, and tapped on the cockpit door.

"Rawlins here."

A voice beyond the door answered. "Just one sec, sir."

The latch clicked and the door swung open. Chet made his way to the left seat and settled in.

"Welcome aboard, sir. Weather looks good until Vegas and then it might get a little bumpy."

Chet had already reviewed the en route weather and knew the new co-pilot wanted to impress him.

"Sounds good. I'll take the first leg, and you get the radios. We can request pushback anytime now."

The co-pilot smiled and nodded.

CHAPTER 30

After a surprisingly restful night, David was up before his four thirty wake-up-call. It was still dark outside, the curtains were drawn closed, and the room was chilly. He took a quick shower, shaved, and dressed. As he pulled on his shoes, the telephone rang. Predictably the call was a computerized voice recording.

"Good morning, this is your wake-up call."

To assure that he would not be disturbed, he left the handset off the cradle. He was rested and completely focused on the task at hand. He was not going to allow anything to interrupt the spiritual battle about to be waged. During the night, his gut feelings had transformed into vision and faith. And now was his time to stand. Hebrews 11:1 defines faith as "being sure of what we hope for and certain of what we do not see."

The knowledge of that Scripture empowered David and as he prepared to talk with God, he recounted his spiritual past—the good parts and the God parts.

I'm a believer. I'm born again. So many years to learn what that really means. So many years spent taking hits from whatever came my way. So many years of not taking authority over the powers, the principalities, and the circumstances that created confusion and unwarranted fear in my life. My God is the God of order, opportunity, creativity, and power, not the God of failure or confusion.

He slid open the nightstand drawer and found the Gideon Bible he had read the night before. Then, as he had done every morning for the past seven years, he let the Bible fall open in his hands. No specific place. No specific book. Wherever it opened, David read. And in doing so, he asked the Holy Spirit to show him, to teach him. That morning, not by coincidence, the Bible opened to Jesus' words in John 14:12–14.

"I tell you the truth, anyone who has faith in me will do what I have been doing. He will do even greater things than these, because I am going to the Father. And I will do whatever you ask in my name, so that the Son may bring glory to the Father. You may ask me for anything in my name, and I will do it."

Those powerful, otherworldly promises lifted and strengthened David's resolve. And as God's Holy Spirit filled him, he understood that the measure of faith within him was enough. His "gut feeling" about this flight had in fact matured into "weather-challenging faith." Now he was ready to pray.

"Lord, You know what's best, and You know my needs, wants, and dreams. With Your permission and in the power of Your Holy Name, I now order that any power, principality, circumstance, or spirit that doesn't agree with Your will for my life be dismissed. Leave now in the name and authority of Jesus. I stand with faith that the weather between here and Las Vegas will allow my flight to proceed without delay or problems. God's will be done in my life and on this trip. Amen."

Within seconds of the amen, Tom knocked on the door.

David walked out carrying his garment bag, and Tom raised an eyebrow.

"If I didn't know better, I'd say there was someone in there with you. It sounded like a conversation was going on."

A part of David wanted to tell Tom about the spiritual battle lines he had just drawn across the sky, but being unsure how he might react, David held back. Instead, he smiled at Tom's query and looked in amusement at his bed–head hair and partial combover.

"Yeah, we're ganging up on you. Let's get to the airport and see what the weather is doing. By the way, are you going to wear your baseball cap?"

With a puzzled look on his sleepy face, Tom answered, "Yeah, it's in the car. Why?"

"Oh nothing, just wondered."

David led the way toward the lobby, hoping Tom could not see that he was about to break out, laughing in part because of Tom's comical appearance but also because of childlike anticipation of things to come.

After a complimentary continental breakfast at the hotel, the two men drove back to the airport under the dark gloom of the offending weather lurking above. It was not raining, but the air was so saturated that Tom occasionally cycled the windshield wipers. Regardless of the no-go feeling in the damp morning air, Tom agreed to follow through with his promise to study the information on the weather computer.

Like a child expecting to find a puppy in a birthday-present box, David was curious to see how the miracles would unfold. In his heart, he knew it was time to stand on the faith and power of his prayerful request. Now was the time to stand on the authority of Jesus' words against the unseen world of principalities, powers, and the weather.

They grabbed some coffee from the airport lobby mini kitchen and huddled around the computer screen, reading encrypted weather forecasts and color-coded weather images. David began to see an opportunity, but only if they left soon.

Of course, Tom saw it too but was not going to acknowledge it—not yet. The freezing levels were at eleven thousand feet, and they could safely make the trip at ten thousand feet, just below the icing conditions. Although it meant flying on instruments in the clouds most of the way to Las Vegas Tom's instrument flying skills were current, and Big Mike was equipped with all the right stuff.

David recognized the window of opportunity but faced the "Tom problem."

Tom sensed David's determination and knew what was coming as David placed his index finger on the computer monitor and tapped the screen at the line containing the icing levels.

"I see it. But Dave, the route of flight will take us over mountains where the lowest altitude for a safe ride is ten thousand feet. Flying any lower means the risk of finding a mountain in the clouds. And remember, the freezing levels are all the way down to eleven thousand feet. If the forecast is wrong, we'll find ourselves in a tight spot, somewhere between heavy ice and hard earth."

David listened intently and responded respectfully. "I know, but it is a window. And I think we can do it. You have the skill, Big Mike has deicing boots, hot props, and I'll be there to help with radios or anything else."

Before he was finished, Tom interjected.

"There's more, Dave. Take a look at that monster sitting over Las Vegas."

David leaned forward and looked closely at the huge red, yellow, and green mass covering the screen where Las Vegas should be.

Green was bad, yellow was worse, and red was almost certain disaster. To be more specific, green was rain with possible turbulence; yellow was heavier rain with potentially severe turbulence; and red was heavy rain with severe turbulence, updrafts, and possible hailstones. David remembered during his weather training when Chet showed him similar weather images and called the red areas "windshield smashin', rivet poppin', wing rippin', airplane killers."

He turned to Tom.

"It's there now, but we won't be near Las Vegas for a couple hours. It will have moved on by then, don't you think?"

Tom surprised David with his response and change of heart.

"Yeah, it probably will. If you want to do this, we better get moving."

David had confidence in Tom, Big Mike, the weather analysis, and their combined flying skills. But there was more going on in his spirit than mere confidence in temporal things. He had prayed. He had taken authority over the situation, and he knew that God's will was assured. There was no doubt. There was no fear. There was no reason to question this window of opportunity. And now Tom was on board.

"Miracle number one," David said to himself.

They were cleared by airport security, allowing them to drive the rental car onto the terminal ramp and next to Big Mike. Condensation was dripping off the wings, which meant the air was saturated with moisture, and icing would definitely be a problem if they got up into the freezing levels or if the freezing levels came down to them.

The sun was up, but the overcast blocked even a hint of where it was in the sky. On the ground, the visibility was about two miles; the surface winds were calm; and the cloud bottoms were reported to be six thousand feet above the airport. Pilot reports, with the acronym PIREPS in weather briefings, had called the tops at fifteen thousand feet and icing at eleven thousand, which meant they would be cruising almost in the middle of the cloud layer and skimming the freezing levels. That was, of course, assuming the PIREPS still applied when they climbed into the soup.

After helping transfer the suitcases and from the car to Big Mike, David returned the rental car, and Tom did the preflight inspection. When David returned, he heard Tom calling from under the right wingtip tank. "Hop in. We've got some water in this one. I'll clear it and see you inside."

David nodded and climbed aboard. After settling into the co-pilot seat, he prayed silently. "Father, here we go."

Before he was finished strapping in, Tom climbed into the pilot's seat and radioed departure control for their clearance. He glanced back into the empty cabin one last time, pulled on the seatbelt and shoulder harness, and handed David the checklist.

"Let's go. And hope that weather briefing is right. If it's not, I'm turning this thing around. Agreed?"

Seeing the confidence in Tom's eyes and having even more confidence in the power of his prayers, David smiled back. "Agreed."

Suddenly the radio came to life. "Cessna Five Three Seven Eight Mike … Phoenix Departure … cleared as filed … contact Ground on one three two point five."

CHAPTER 31

With the engines at full power, Tom released the brakes, and Big Mike lurched forward, rolling down the centerline of Phoenix Sky Harbor Runway Seven Right. The earth slipped smoothly away and when there was not enough runway remaining for an emergency landing, Tom retracted the landing gear. He trimmed for an eight-hundred-feet-per-minute climb rate and held the runway heading, waiting for course change instructions from air traffic control.

As Tom pulled the RPM, props, and fuel mixtures back to cruise-climb settings, David felt the familiar yet strange sensation of climbing in spite of engine sounds that suddenly seemed too quiet for the task. The radio invaded the cockpit, breaking their silent concentration.

"Five Three Seven Eight Mike … Phoenix Departure … turn left heading three one zero … maintain five thousand feet … expect higher in one zero miles."

As Big Mike banked and climbed on the assigned departure heading, the upscale community of Scottsdale and the Taliesin West School of Architecture came into view below. The school was founded in the 1930s by world-renowned architect Frank Lloyd Wright and held memories for David.

As his view of the campus slipped under the airplane, he remembered visiting Taliesin on a field trip with fellow architectural students more than thirty years ago. At that time, he had no idea what lay ahead. If someone had said he would be president of his own architectural firm, riding in his own airplane with a corporate pilot at the helm, and following God's lead through the weather and with direct communication with Him, David would have laughed in disbelief. His daydreaming was interrupted by a voice over the radio.

"Seven Eight Mike ... Phoenix Departure ... maintain current heading ... climb to one zero thousand feet."

David confirmed the instructions.

"Up to one zero thousand ... Seven Eight Mike."

Immediately above, the solid overcast cloud layer awaited, ready to envelop them in the white and gray world of no visible horizon, no visual cues, and no material evidence of the earth below. The experience of climbing up into the base of a cloud layer, leveling off, and losing all references to the earth was unique and unforgettable. Regardless of what window they looked through, there would be nothing to see beyond the nose or the wings. There would be no visible horizon and no ground references—only their flying skills, Big Mike's instruments, and the inexorable pull of gravity if the engines failed. Survival and success were dependent on their skill, faith, and God's hand protecting them from the hard reality of the earth below.

As the anticipation of slipping into the clouds grew, David felt God's assurance and a reminder that He has always been with him.

God whispered, *Remember those years spent not seeing My influence in your life. I Am there. Remember immersing yourself in worldly things to avoid thinking of Me. I Am there. Remember, David, I Am the great I Am. I Am with you now.*

Those words strengthened him and, at the same time, brought forward memories of his past, a past filled with wasted time and energy in a worldly attempt to live in denial of the power and presence of God. He remembered living the lie while continuing to struggle with whatever hit him, good or bad. Without God in his life, the world's manmade theories, misguided teachings, and burdensome religions only frustrated and confused. Like flying in the clouds without training, skill, or instruments—or faith.

———

Meanwhile, thirty five thousand feet over Oklahoma, Chet patched into the onboard satellite phone and called David to tell him that he had gotten the New York to Las Vegas run. When he discovered that neither David nor Tom was answering his phone, he called David's office.

"Architect's office," Jenny crisply announced.

"Hi, this is Chet Rawlins. Is Mr. Adams in?"

She quickly answered, passing on the information she had overheard when Tom and David were discussing the trip two days earlier. "No, Mr. Rawlins. Tom has flown Mr. Adams to Phoenix. They left yesterday morning. As I understand it, Mr. Adams is going to fly commercial from there to Las Vegas, and Tom is going to wait in Phoenix until some bad weather passes."

"Thanks, I'll try his cell phone later."

He ended the call and sighed deeply.

"Way to go, Tom. Keep it safe buddy."

———

At that very moment, Tom and David were flying on instruments, in the clouds, somewhere south of Flagstaff, Arizona.

CHAPTER 32

Most pilots grow accustomed to the challenge of watching the instrument panel bounce and shake while the seatbelt prevents them from getting a head slammed against the cockpit ceiling. Beyond keeping your cool in a rough ride, the other challenges include dialing in radio frequencies and adjusting instruments, all of which jump away from your fingertips every time the airplane punches through another wall of unstable air. It's like driving a road strewn with unavoidable potholes but with a three-dimensional component. And the potholes are invisible.

But not so in Big Mike. The smooth ride was the next clue that David's prayers were being answered. Miracle number two.

After fifteen minutes on course and in the clouds, Tom looked at David and laughed as they heard a Las Vegas-bound Southwest Airlines pilot call air traffic control requesting a lower altitude due to turbulence. Somewhere above them, the Boeing 737 was blasting through the bumpy sky at over five hundred miles per hour. Yet they were enjoying a smooth ride as the deep, steady drone of Big Mike's engines dutifully pulled them through the wet clouds toward Las Vegas at two hundred and twenty miles per hour.

Having flown commercial more often than he would have liked, David remembered flights with passengers groping for spilled peanuts or balancing sloshing drinks as the airplane suddenly dropped and bumped. And for those sitting in window seats, there was the added stress of watching the wings wag up and down while hoping they stayed attached to the airplane.

The ride was smooth, and they were just below the freezing level. If ice did develop, the electric prop heaters and pneumatic boots along the leading edges of the wings and tail would come into play. But knowing the limitations of those systems, Tom understood that if ice began to build, they would start looking for warmer air. Or, as promised, he would turn the thing around.

Leveling off just south of Sedona, Tom switched on the autopilot and watched for ice on his side of the airplane. David dialed in the radio-frequency changes, tracked their location relative to available airports, and watched for ice on his side of the airplane. He was confident, yet his mind tried to challenge the faith in his heart. Just how close they were to the icing zone was clearly shown on the temperature gauge mounted on David's side of the instrument panel.

One degree above freezing. Close but no ice yet. Miracle number three. No ice yet. Yet! Where did that come from? Weak faith? If I have faith, I can't doubt. Can I?

As David pondered the "yet" thoughts, he noticed the dull gray outside growing a little whiter. They had been in the air for an hour and forty-two minutes, which meant the southern portion of the Grand Canyon was somewhere below and Las Vegas ahead in the distance. But for the clouds.

CHAPTER 33

Monotony. The best short description of a long, cloud-shrouded flight.

A little prayer floated through David's mind as the gray sky turned dirty white.

We trust you, Lord. Thank you for the adventure.

Suddenly, the dirty white exploded with color as Big Mike burst out of the clouds into clear air and unlimited visibility. Directly ahead, a huge rainbow ring appeared with Big Mike's nose pointed directly at the center, like a well-placed arrow toward a bull's-eye. Miracle number four.

David wanted to say something but could not speak as the surreal intensity of crystal-clear blue sky, cream-brown desert floor, and the explosion of light and color blasted into sight. In the split second it took for them to slip free of the clouds, they were transported from the gray world of visual sensory deprivation into a world flooded with colors and natural beauty, into the visual richness of God's sun-drenched creation.

After adjusting his eyes to the bright new surroundings, David forced himself to look away from the amazing rainbow ring and out the side window where the huge gash of the Grand Canyon wound deep and imposing into the earth ten thousand feet below.

They had flown this route many times before and each time the natural colors of the canyon, although impressive, had shown subdued and earth toned in comparison. The normally muted colors were intensified into rich reds, yellows, creams, browns, and greens as the morning sun burned against the south-facing canyon walls and reflected back at them.

Following the canyon forward, David's eyes returned to the rainbow ring still hanging in the air dead ahead.

"My God, more color and we're flying straight toward it."

Tom answered. "This is amazing."

The rich, illuminated colors of the Grand Canyon morning and the prismatic purity of the rainbow ring set against the crisp blue sky turned David's thoughts to praise.

Thank You, God, for being with us. Thank You for the beauty of Your creation. Thank You for answering prayers. And thank You for my life with You.

David felt a childlike energy fill him as he experienced the wonder and intimacy of celebrating God's creation with Him. Yet at the same time, deep in his spirit, he was confident and mature, knowing that this was the direct result of prayer and faith. The results of "being sure of what we hope for and certain of what we do not see."

In his heart, David cried, *Thank you, Father!*

He remembered the thrill of his earthly daddy tossing him into the air, catching him and then tossing him up again. And each time little David would squeal, "Again, Daddy, again!"

Strapped into his seat and flying through the air, his spirit, like a child, called out to his heavenly Father, *Again, Father, again!*

David was grateful that Tom was flying because he was lost in the spiritual thrill of God's love, awestruck by the beauty and reflecting on the prayer and faith that brought victory over ice, calmed the turbulence, and gave safety from danger and courage to Tom. The sound of a radio call from air traffic control snapped David back to earth.

"Five Three Seven Eight Mike... Las Vegas Approach ... descend to eight thousand feet ... altimeter two niner niner eight ... report Stratosphere in sight."

The Stratosphere Casino Hotel Tower is a visual marker for pilots approaching Runways One Nine Left and Right. Its location and height make it the perfect landmark for entering the traffic pattern.

Tom responded. "Las Vegas Approach ... Five Three Seven Eight Mike ... down to eight ... no contact."

David looked toward Tom, and said, "I never hear you say "no joy."

Tom smiled, and answered, "no contact is American ... "no joy" sounds British. I prefer American. Either way, they know we can't see it yet."

Tom eased back the throttles to begin the descent and to stage cool the engines. The weather briefing had been right: The storm cell they had seen on the weather radar image appeared to be sitting over Las Vegas, obstructing their ability to see city skyline and, more importantly, the Stratosphere.

CHAPTER 34

Tom and David sat in silence, isolated by the mental and spiritual reality of God's presence pouring into their minds and hearts as they roared through the sky toward the rainbow. And although the cockpit was filled with the sounds and sights of manmade flight, the intense natural beauty and glorious halo like rainbow outshone anything they had ever seen or experienced. Tom was awakened to God's real and active presence, and David's heart filled with confidence and peace.

As they held the westerly heading toward Las Vegas and continued to cruise at the assigned altitude of eight thousand feet, David saw the headwaters of Lake Mead and the Colorado River come into view. The southwest boundaries of the Grand Canyon slid away behind them and, off to the right, the river snaked north, disappearing into the hills.

The rainbow ring was still ahead, but as they made their descent, it morphed from a ring into a rainbow arch with the right foot on the hills to the north and the left foot sitting directly ahead between Big Mike and the dark clouds. Miracle number five.

David had settled down from the spiritual high and helped Tom with the charts and checklists. According to the moving map, the heading indicator, and the card compass, the Stratosphere Casino Tower was directly ahead. Knowing that they were exactly on course, David and Tom peered through the windshield and looked for the white shaft of the Stratosphere somewhere in the base of the dark clouds.

Tom dialed Com 2, the second radio, to the Automated Terminal Information Service, or ATIS, frequency, a prerecorded broadcast that, among other things, gives airport wind speed, wind direction, ceiling heights, and visibility. According to the ATIS, the winds were straight down the runway at ten to fifteen miles per hour and the visibility was five miles. The storm cell was moving north but still hiding the city.

David squinted and, in the base of the dark cloud, saw a small white shaft projecting from the ground directly into the center of the rainbow's foot. Miracle number six.

"Tom, do you see something in the base of the rainbow? Like maybe the Stratosphere?"

Tom leaned forward in his seat, lifted up his sunglasses, and smiled.

"Well, I'll be."

Before David could respond, Tom keyed the mic button.

"Las Vegas Approach ... Five Three Seven Eight Mike has Stratosphere in sight."

In a hurried response, the controller radioed back.

"Seven Eight Mike ... Las Vegas Approach ... cleared into Bravo airspace ... expect Runway One Niner Right ... contact Tower on one one niner point niner ... good day."

As they began the descent, with the Stratosphere dead ahead, the rainbow began to move. David's mind and heart leaped in anticipation.

"Here we go again. God is up to something."

Tom did not respond.

As they descended and banked left to line up with the runway, the rainbow moved with them until it rested on the threshold of Runway One Nine Right. Their runway. Miracle number seven.

Tom briefly looked at David, but neither man could speak. Then, as Big Mike glided over Tropicana Avenue and the airport perimeter fence, the rainbow faded and was gone.

Tom was silent in part due to concentrating on the landing but also shocked and amazed at what they just experienced. He wanted to talk. He wanted to ask. He wanted to know more. But not yet.

They continued down the last few feet of the final approach at one hundred twenty miles per hour and, at less than one foot off the pavement, Tom pulled back the remaining power to the engines, and glided Big Mike onto the runway centerline. After a short rollout, they took the first high speed-exit, and Tom radioed ground control requesting permission to taxi to the executive air terminal. Other than Tom's radio communication with ground control, no words were spoken. It was too amazing, too wonderful, and too powerful to be a coincidence or fluke of nature.

Ahead they saw the airport follow-me van pull onto the taxiway, David's cue to get ready for his last scheduled meeting. Then they could head for home. But David still could not speak, mostly because of the huge grin that seemed permanently stuck to his face.

Neither could Tom speak—but for different reasons.

CHAPTER 35

They rode in silence in the back of the white shuttle van for the short ride from Big Mike to the terminal. There was so much to say, but neither man knew where to start or what to say.

The aerial dance with the rainbow burned deep personal and spiritual impressions into each of them, deep enough to defy the mere use of words, personal to the point of intimacy, and so spiritually powerful that flesh and mind were forced to surrender to heart. They would ponder and digest its full meaning for the remainder of their earthly lives, however long that would be.

David was filled with the joy and confidence that comes from a father-and-son wrestling match, full of mischief, laughter, trust, and awe.

Tom was filled with questions. Questions stimulated by the very real awareness that God does exist and that He does interact with His kids. He had seen it more than once in David's life, but now it was more than just an interesting, almost explainable coincidence. Now it was very real. And now it included Tom.

But even more daunting, he questioned his standing with God. He was raised by a family that went to church religiously and gave money to needy causes. And he had done those same religious things with his own young family. His mind was filled with questions in need of answers, questions his heart knew had everlasting significance. If he could have held back any longer, he would. But he could not.

"Dave. Have you got a few minutes before you leave?"

David jumped at the chance to answer, having hoped deep within his spirit that this exchange would happen someday.

"You bet. Let's go to the pilots' lounge."

An airport lineman brought David's rental car and left the keys with the front desk while Tom and David sat alone in the comfortable chairs in the pilots' lounge. David opened the conversation with the sincerity of heart that God had placed there for Tom to receive.

"I don't want to sound preachy, Tom, but there are some things I've wanted to tell you for a long time."

He paused to look at his watch then continued.

"I need to leave soon, but let me say this ..."

Tom nervously interrupted.

"I know. It's OK. We can talk about it after you get back."

"No, this is important. I'll make it to the meeting. God is doing something with us. With you."

"You think?" Tom mumbled, feeling sorry that his words sounded sarcastic.

David paused briefly before continuing. He had wanted to talk to Tom about God since bringing him on board. The talk that could ruin his working relationship with Tom. The talk that much of modern American culture has begun to admonish as "not politically correct" between employer and employee. Looking straight into Tom's eyes and seeing the spiritual hunger there, David began.

"As believers, we know that God is with us even though we can't physically see Him. We know in our hearts that He gives us life experiences and a spiritual history that guides and protects us through our lives. Like a caring father, He arranges things around us for our protection and growth, usually without our knowing. To assume that luck was on our side or that an interesting coincidence had occurred misses the mark. God loves us regardless of our inattention. Regardless of apathy and our spiritual disregard. Regardless of our manmade religious practices. He loves us and has a plan for our lives. More importantly Tom, He loves you and He has a plan for your life."

Tom heard every word, many of them stinging deep within. His mind struggled, fighting against the conviction that poured from his heart into his consciousness.

How had I missed it? How have I not been aware of something so obvious? Why had religion betrayed me? Should I have even opened this door? Life was so much simpler with God in a box.

Backing away from things that he was unsure of is what Tom had done all his life, and the old habit was kicking in again.

"Yeah, I know, Dave. Let me think about all that. You go on to the meeting and I'll see you after."

Feeling burdened with unsubstantiated guilt and certain that he had said too much too fast, David surrendered to his fears and agreed.

"OK. I'll see you in a few hours."

They parted in silence, Tom intending to go to the front desk and to make Big Mike's fuel order and David to his last worldly obligation.

But the spiritual battle raging inside Tom prevented him from leaving the room or from doing anything but sitting back down alone in the pilots' lounge. He sank into the worn, overstuffed leather chair and bent over, head down, with his face in his hands and his eyes beginning to tear. Memories flooded the room, some laced with condemnation and others wrapped in fear.

I've never done anything that's really bad. I never killed anybody. I never cheated on Margie. I never did anything really bad.

Unannounced and coming from deep inside Tom's youthful memories, pieces of the seemingly forgotten Apostles Creed began to play. It was one of the many memorizations required when he was confirmed into his mother's church. And now it flowed in broken pieces into his consciousness like a rediscovered, partially damaged recording.

I believe in one God the Father Almighty, Maker of heaven and earth … And of all things visible and invisible … One Lord Jesus Christ, the only begotten Son of God … crucified under Pontius Pilate … He suffered and was buried … and ascended into heaven … He shall come again with glory, to judge both the living and the dead.

Attached to the memories, and new to Tom, was assurance that God loved him. Assurance that the past was forgiven and forgotten, never to threaten again. Assurance that he was not alone. Assurance that God was with him and would always be with him.

He wiped his eyes, leaned back in the chair, and rested there, looking up at the ceiling. He began to feel the soul-filling warmth of peace and confidence that only those who answer God's call can experience. As he shifted in the chair, intending to stand, his right hand brushed against a book sitting on the lamp table next to a dirty black glass ashtray. He brushed the ashtray aside and picked up the book to discover that it was an old, brown leather Bible. The cover was faded. The edges were cracked, as happens with old dry leather, and the yellowed pages were stained and tattered from age and use. Tom had never read the Bible, only the prayer book his mother had forced on him. Not knowing where to start but drawn to it as light in a dark tunnel, he simply let the Bible fall open in his hands and began reading the verses that lay before him.

John 14:11: Believe me when I say that I am in the Father and the Father is in me; or at least believe on the evidence of the miracles themselves.

In disbelief, his mind attempted to reject the scriptural discovery as weird or coincidental, but his heart took over and his spirit continued to be filled with God's Holy Spirit. The same Holy Spirit whose name he had so religiously, so dutifully, so casually recited in congregational prayers and songs. At God's urging, he unknowingly obeyed and turned a few pages, causing the Bible to open to the next gentle lesson awaiting him. Seeming to shine from the wrinkled pages, Tom read at first to himself and then again softly aloud to the empty room.

1 Peter 1:8: Though you have not seen him, you love him; and even though you do not see him now, you believe in him and are filled with an inexpressible and glorious joy.

"Yes, I do and yes, I am!" Tom declared as he stood with his face turned up, still wet with tears, and feeling much taller than his earthly five-foot-eight-inch frame. Still holding the Bible with his index finger preserving the pages that had just empowered him, he continued reading the next lesson God had for him.

1 Peter 2: 1–2: Therefore, rid yourselves of all malice and all deceit, hypocrisy, envy, and slander of every kind. Like newborn babies, crave pure spiritual milk, so that by it you may grow up in your salvation, now that you have tasted that the Lord is good.

The power of those scriptures sunk deep into Tom's heart, causing him to sit back down and, with the new-found confidence of a son speaking to his loving Father, he prayed.

"Thank You, Father. Teach me, show me. I am Yours."

God's response clearly and gently flowed through Tom's heart and mind.

"Yes, you are in Me and I am in you. I will be with you always."

CHAPTER 36

David parked the rental car near the warehouse door. The only other car around was also a rental. He hoped it was Cliff's. The door was unlocked and as David walked in, Cliff called to him.

"Dave. Over here."

Cliff was standing next to one of three empty box trailers, each with the rear doors opened.

"Hello, Cliff. When did you get here?"

"About an hour ago. I got the 6:45 flight on Southworst."

"Oh, come on. Southwest is a good airline, as airlines go."

"Yeah, I know. But it was real bumpy and I hate that."

David chuckled.

"Really? 6:45 and bumpy."

Cliff looked puzzled.

"Yeah, why?"

"Oh nothing. Just curious."

David set his briefcase on the deck of a nearby box trailer and spun the locks, releasing the latches.

"Cliff, your job is to load these trailers with the material staged along the wall. Use local labor and pay them in cash."

Cliff looked around the large warehouse and saw a number chalked on the floor in front of each stack. The boxes were of all sizes, the smallest the size of a microwave and the largest the size of a single bed mattress.

David continued. "The number on the floor matches the number marked in chalk on the trailer. Load them accordingly. When they're loaded, call me and we'll set the shipment dates. Trailer one goes to Goodyear, two to Albuquerque, and three to Utah. The departures are based on your readiness."

"Goodyear is ready and Utah is close, about four weeks out."

David sighed in relief and handed Cliff a spiral-bound notebook.

"These are diagrams of where in the chambers to place the stuff before you seal them off. Do you think the general contractors suspect anything?"

Cliff chuckled and took the notebook from David.

"The guy in Tucson never leaves the trailer except to get somethin' from the roach coach. But the G.C. in Chandler does poke around a little."

"Watch him." David responded in a cautious tone, then continued. "The notebooks also have the specs you need to seal off the lower level. I need you to drill and set the new wall rebar in epoxy and pour the walls sixteen inches thick."

David hurriedly closed his briefcase and, without looking, gave the tumblers a quick spin.

"Any questions?"

Cliff raised an eyebrow and whistled.

"Wow, twelve inches? The perimeters are only eight-inch block."

"Yes. They have earth backfill. These walls won't."

CHAPTER 37

"Come on! My shift is done. I want to go home!"

The dispatcher looked up from the paperwork semi-organized in stacks atop his deck.

"Sorry, but I need you to fuel Five Three Seven Eight Mike before you clock out. Looks like we missed it. The fuel order says fill the mains. On a 421, those are the tip tanks. Get to it and you can go home."

With an exaggerated arm swing and grunting four-letter sounds, the lineman snatched the keys from the smudged pegboard.

"And I guess I'm stuck with this piece of crap. Where are the new trucks?"

The dispatcher responded without looking up from his paperwork.

"They're at maintenance getting purged and loaded. Now get going before the front desk calls it in again."

The lineman intentionally let the door slam behind him as he left the office. Across the ramp was the waiting fuel truck. Although he knew it had not been used for several days, he did not drain the fuel sump or bleed fuel/water separator. Instead, he climbed into the soiled cab, fired up the engine, and ground the truck into gear. As he rolled out of the fuel yard and onto the ramp, he realized that he did not know where the airplane was tied down. He radioed the dispatcher and spoke in an exasperated tone of voice.

"Dispatch, where in hell is 5378 Mike parked? Over."

"Thought you might want to know. Transient, Row Three. Out."

He found the white Cessna 421 and confirmed that the tail number matched the fuel order. As he climbed out of the cab, he noticed the faded American flag on the tall vertical stabilizer. He mumbled to himself and Big Mike, grumbling more at the condition of his life than the age of the airplane.

"Old bird."

After he attached the static ground cable to the tab under the wing, he set the stepladder next to the right tip tank, reached up, popped open the fuel cap latch, and twisted. The cap popped loose and he set it down on the side of the tank, letting it hang there by the safety chain. The gusting wind buffeted against him as he eased the fuel nozzle into the throat of the streamlined, sharklike tank.

With yet another missed opportunity to bleed the truck's fuel/water separator, he squeezed the handle and Avgas began to flow. Before he discovered that the tank had already been topped off by the previous shift, six ounces of water flowed through the nozzle with the fuel. And by the time he removed the nozzle, the water had settled into the sump beneath the tip tank's fuel pump. He cursed under his breath and replaced the cap, completely unaware of the fuel contamination he had just caused. As he stood watching the static line auto wind onto the spool, he looked up and yelled into the brisk wind, "What else can go wrong? I didn't need to do this!"

He was not going to radio the dispatcher with this one. He would rather tell him face to face and enjoy the reward of reporting the screw-up in person.

CHAPTER 38

David found Tom sitting in the lobby, ready to go. He walked up and tossed him the keys to the rental car.

"Tom. Let's get out of here."

Tom responded with a teasing grin, and David took the bait. "You OK?"

"Yeah, I'm good. I'm real good."

"I see that. What's up, Tom? You got something to tell me?"

Tom looked down at his feet and then glanced around the busy lobby.

"I did it. I talked to Him. I got …"

His voice trembled as he struggled to continue. Then he looked up at David and, with eyes beginning to tear, he managed to get out the rest of the good news. "He is real … God is real. I have Jesus in my life … I did it."

Both men were tearing as they stood face to face, spiritually isolated from the activity of the airport lobby. David wanted to speak but was not sure what to say. He held out his hand, intending to congratulate him with a traditional handshake. But instead, Tom reached forward and embraced him in a manly hug. David did what most men do in such circumstances and patted Tom soundly on the back a few times. No one in the crowded room noticed. Tom quickly released David and stepped back, embarrassed by his actions.

"Sorry, Dave, that was weird."

"No, Tom, that wasn't weird. That was you and God and me. There is so much ahead of you. So much. I know in my heart you've only begun."

Tom nodded in agreement.

"What do you say we head home?"

"Can we? It's pretty windy out there."

David had anticipated a typical pre-departure briefing, but Tom clearly wanted to get airborne.

"Yeah, it'll be bumpy, but we've been in worse. There's a marine layer moving into San Diego, so we may have to shoot an approach. If we get out of here in the next half hour, we might beat it."

Then he changed the subject. "There was more water in the right tank. I got it out, but we may have a bad O ring on the cap. I'll have it checked when we get home."

David picked up his briefcase. "Then let's go for it Tom."

"Sounds good, we're fueled and good to go. I did the preflight already, right after the fuel truck left."

On the ride out to Big Mike, the van was forced to wait for a fuel truck that appeared to have just pulled away from the airplane. But Tom was not concerned. He had watched the fueling and cleared the tanks of water more than three hours before. As he watched the truck rumble by, he assumed it had fueled one of the airplanes parked nearby.

David watched, too, and noticed the driver shaking his head and talking to himself as he tossed a large metal clipboard onto the truck's dashboard.

CHAPTER 39

The sun was low and resting on the Red Rock hills to the west as they pulled up to the airplane. Tom quickly hopped out of the van.

"Dave, I'll get us ready if you can load the stuff?"

"No problem," David answered as he waited for the driver to open the rear doors of the van.

Tom rushed to pull the wheel chocks and release the tie-down chains as Big Mike rocked against the gusting surface winds. He tossed the chains and chocks to the ground, away from the props, and climbed into the cabin. David boarded right behind him with his briefcase in hand. The van driver handed David the suitcases, waved, and said, "Good flight, Godspeed."

David closed the clamshell door and headed for the co-pilot's seat, gratefully praying. *God, it's good to be heading home. Thank You for all You do, Lord. Thank You for Tom.*

Tom was already strapped into the pilot's seat and on the radio filing a flight plan when David slipped into the co-pilot's seat. There was an unfamiliar urgency in the air to rush through the pre-departure checklist. David could feel it as he watched Tom fire up the engines and radio ground control.

"Las Vegas Ground … Cessna Five Three Seven Eight Mike at Executive … ready to taxi with information Uniform."

After a brief pause, the radio crackled back. "Cessna Seven Eight Mike … confirm you have information Uniform."

Tom responded as he dialed the tower frequency into Com 2, "Affirmative ... Seven Eight Mike."

"Seven Eight Mike, taxi to one niner right via taxiway Alpha ... hold short ... when ready to go, contact Tower ... good flight."

Tom clicked the mic button. "Alpha to one niner right ... hold short."

The gusty winds continued to buffet Big Mike as they taxied the short distance to the runway. Tonight, for the moment, they were the only airplane departing from One Nine Right. In anticipation of a quick clearance, Tom checked the magnetos and rushed through the pre-takeoff checklist as they taxied. And just as he expected, when they neared the runway, the tower came over the radio.

"Seven Eight Mike ... we have departures on the intersecting runway ... can you expedite?"

"Affirmative ... Seven Eight Mike ready to go ... one niner right."

Tom's quick response got an equally quick clearance. "Seven Eight Mike cleared for takeoff ... expedite please."

Tom pushed the throttles, props, and mixtures forward. "Seven Eight Mike rolling."

The gusty evening winds blew on an angle across the runway, causing a quartering headwind that pushed against the right side of the airplane. To stay on track, Tom aggressively worked the rudder pedals as they wandered left and right off the centerline. The moment the wheels lifted off the runway, Big Mike was blown to the left and Tom quickly corrected by flying a fifteen-degree right crab angle to hold them on track with the runway centerline as they struggled skyward.

"Man, is it bumpy!" David exclaimed, not expecting a response.

Big Mike managed to climb, but the gusts reduced the normal climb rate by half as downdrafts caused periods of zero vertical speed, resulting in a series of stepped ascents. As they soared over the intersection of Runway Two Five, Tom lifted the gear lever up and mumbled, "I hope they appreciate it."

The two men looked at each other for a brief moment and Tom smiled first. "We're off. How about going through the checklist with me?"

David nodded and smiled back. "Deal."

Everything seemed normal, except for the bumps and buffeting caused by wind gusts, until Tom pulled the power back to cruise-climb settings. Although the change in engine sounds was familiar, there was a distinctly different feel in the controls, and a subtle vibration was coming from the right side.

"Damn!" Tom shouted.

"What?" David shouted back, knowing something was wrong as he heard the change in wind and engine sounds. "What, Tom?"

"Look out your window. We're losing power on that engine! Can you see anything? Smoke, fire? Anything?"

"I can't tell, what does the …"

David's quick response was halted by the sight a shadowlike puff of smoke slipping out of the cowling and the huge three-bladed propeller spooling down to a dead stop. Before he could verbalize what his disbelieving eyes were seeing, Tom shouted, "We've lost it. We've lost that engine. Help me with the left rudder! We've got to keep the nose straight. Got to raise that dead engine. Damn!"

While David jammed the rudder pedal down to help keep Big Mike under control, Tom feathered the right engine, cranked in rudder trim, and pushed the levers of the left engine to maximum power. The yoke in David's lap was turned almost to the stops, confirming that most of the aileron authority was needed to keep the airplane from rolling inverted. No climb could be nursed from the single roaring engine, and they were rapidly losing altitude as the gusts pushed Big Mike down in regular intervals. In less aggressive winds, they could have made it back to the airport, but the gusting downdrafts had increased in force and frequency, completely overpowering their efforts.

David shouted, "We've got to turn back to the airport!"

Tom shook his head and answered, "Can't ... can't. We're too low. Look for a place to set it down!" Then he pointed ahead and repeated, "Find us a place to set this thing down. I'll tell Las Vegas!"

"Mayday! Mayday! Mayday! Cessna Seven Eight Mike lost engine ... two miles south of airport ... forced landing ... Mayday! Mayday! Mayday!"

Tom finished the radio call and shouted, "What you got?" His voice was firm and determined as he struggled to maintain control of the buffeting, underpowered airplane.

David confirmed what Tom had already determined.

"We can't use Las Vegas Boulevard. Too much traffic, but..." David pointed toward a place he hoped might work. "There's a construction site a little to the right. Can we get there?"

Tom quickly responded by pulling back the power, feathering the engine, and closing the remaining fuel valves.

"OK, we're a seven-thousand-pound glider. Tighten your shoulder harness 'til it hurts, and take everything out of your shirt pockets. We're going to leave the gear up and belly it in. Man, I hate these gusts! I've got the airplane. You just brace yourself and pray!"

David watched the earth rise to meet them.

God! This can't be happening. There's nothing ahead but dirt and brush. No runway. No roadway. No soft grassy field. God, this is bad!

He closed his eyes just for a few seconds, his mind swimming with a mixture of memories, faces, and prayers.

At one hundred feet above the ground, Tom switched off all the electrical power. The radios, the intercom, and the instrument panel went dead. Then at five feet off the ground, with his head pressed back against the headrest, he pulled back on the yoke and lifted the nose to slow their fall. The wings buffeted one last time, just before the tail hit the ground. Big Mike's belly skidded onto the sandy, rock-strewn surface at one hundred miles per hour, sending flumes of dirt, rock, and dust up and over the careening airplane.

David saw the lower propeller blade on his side fold back as it dragged along the ground. Then, suddenly, the right wingtip hit a mound of dirt and rocks. Out the corner of his eye, he saw the tip tank separate from the wing and tumble out of sight, spewing fuel. The impact turned the airplane slightly, causing it to skid and bounce on an angle to the direction of travel and increasing the impact damage to the nose and windshield on Tom's side.

David's seatbelt and shoulder harness dug into his body with every bounce and jolt. He gripped the sides of his seat and braced for more.

CHAPTER 40

The sound of a blade slicing through the air like a spinning propeller ripped past David's head and legs. And with the deadly sound, he heard a mixture of sporadic hissing and screaming. He squinted to see through the brightness that filled the dust-shrouded cockpit and then quickly pushed his head back against the headrest in response to a gleaming blade suddenly flashing by, inches from his face. Believing he was hearing and seeing the demise of the disintegrating airplane, he squeezed his eyes closed and braced for death's final blow.

Then slowly and completely contrary to the horrific circumstances and frightening noises that surrounded him, faint feelings of protection and security washed over David. With his head turned slightly to the right, he cautiously opened his eyes and saw that everything had slowed down. With the shift in time and speed, he noticed that the sounds had also changed to lower, more recognizable frequencies. Although the slicing noises were still incredibly loud and dangerously close, they now sounded more like voices.

And the brilliance of the light had changed in intensity and location. Now instead of one bright, blinding light he saw three separate lights, one on each side of him and one in front. The lights were in the form of men but taller—much taller. Their radiant white robes hung so close to David, he could almost touch them. All three were facing away from him as they stood shoulder to shoulder, creating a protective barrier between David and whatever they were protecting him from. Each one held a sword in a two-handed grip and swung the gleaming blades in smooth, powerful arches.

Seeing but hardly believing his eyes, David processed the new reality before him.

Oh God ... these are angels. And the sound I hear ... what is that?

He concentrated on the sounds while he watched the blades carve through the air, beginning to hear and understand. The sounds the blades emitted were words and phrases, like Bible verses. And each slice of a blade was followed by hissing and hideous screeching. The angels moved and swayed as they stood firm, continuing the battle and cleaving their enemies with the powerful blades. And as they moved, David could see dark forms just beyond the angelic perimeter, moving, reaching, trying to slip past the angels.

One after another, they attempted to reach through, intent on grabbing him. But each evil attempt was cut off by the angels as their swords sliced through the offending creatures, causing the dark forms to explode, emitting hellish sounds, and evaporate before David's startled eyes. The angel on his left swung at something approaching and, as he did, the blade sung out.

"He is the light of the world."

Then with another arching swing.

"Whoever follows Him will never walk in darkness."

The angel in front of David followed with a curving blow that sent two of the things to oblivion. And over the hellish noise of the battle, he heard the blade proclaim a resonating message.

"He gives them eternal life, and they shall never perish."

There was a brief pause in the fight and suddenly the angel in front of David thrust his sword again. The blade jutted forward and swung upward. He pointed the blade straight up above his head with his powerful arms extended. As he raised the sword, it sung out.

"No one can snatch them out of His hand."

David struggled to accept the reality of the battle for his life. Then slowly and confidently, the angel at his right turned and looked over his shoulder. At first, fear gripped David as the angel locked eyes with him. Then, gradually, the stern look of the angelic warrior relaxed, changing into the face of a protector and much-needed friend. David felt frozen in place as he watched the angel reach toward him, slowly moving his massive open hand toward David's chest.

"Don't be afraid. The battle is won. Today, you will be in Paradise."

As the angelic hand pressed over David's heart, the light around him intensified until there was only white and all sound slowly faded away, dissolving into serene silence.

CHAPTER 41

"We need foam out here. Fuel's leakin' out of both wings. Get on the radio and see where in hell they are. ASAP! And I need access to the cabin. Now!"

The fire chief turned to the young paramedic standing next to him.

"If I can get you in there before the foam goes down, you good with that?"

"Yeah, get me in there. The engines are pretty much buried. That's probably why she didn't burn."

The paramedic looked toward the aft section of the wreckage, the only part not covered in dirt and construction debris, and watched as two firemen smashed the window in the cabin door. They reached inside through the opening and released the latch, allowing the small upper section to swing open. But the crash had jammed the lower section, holding it firmly in place. While they worked with pry bars and axes to break the lower section free, the paramedic scrambled up the dirt mound next to the fuselage. He pushed his medical kit toward one of the firemen.

"Hold this!"

Then he turned to the other fireman.

"Give me a boost."

He scrambled through the small opening and turned to grab the medical kit. It dragged though the opening as he pulled on the strap and the firemen pushed from the outside.

"Thanks guys."

He turned toward the cockpit and clicked on his helmet-mounted led light. The smell of dust, fuel, and blood hung in the air. Two suitcases were jammed in the aisle between the seats, and a briefcase was belted to the cabin seat behind the co-pilot. He crawled forward past the empty seats.

As he reached the narrow opening into the cockpit, he heard a faint moan and shouted into his shoulder-mounted walkie-talkie.

"I've got a live one ... maybe two."

He hoped the other paramedic could hear him over the noise of the Bobcat working on the dirt embankment jammed against the fuselage.

Tom was unconscious. His head slumped forward and to the left, with blood covering his face and chest. His hair was matted with blood from a gash in his scalp. Both arms were pressed onto his lap and pinned there by the instrument panel that had pushed back on impact with the embankment.

Quickly, the paramedic retrieved a compress and tape from the medical kit and tightly wrapped Tom's head, hoping the compress would slow the bleeding long enough to extract him from the wreckage. Then he turned to the co-pilot's seat and saw David's body firmly held in place by the seatbelt and shoulder harness. He sat erect with his head tilted back against the bulkhead, face turned up and eyes closed.

"I've got no pulse or respiration on the right. Let's get the left seat out first."

The fire chief heard the paramedic's walkie-talkie broadcast and barked out instructions to the crew.

"Get the saw and jaws up to the front! Pilot's side! And move the Bobcat to the other side."

Just then, he saw the foam truck pull up. He waved to the driver and pointed to the ground behind the wing.

"Both wings!" The cacophony generated by the massive collection of power tools and equipment almost overpowered the sound of his voice.

As the rescue team extracted Tom through the newly cut hole in the side of the fuselage, none of them were aware of the tall figures moving with them. Their movements were fluid and confident as they positioned themselves for battle, one a few feet from Tom's unconscious body and eight more surrounding the ambulance in shoulder-to-shoulder formation facing outward. As they scanned the perimeter, the angels could see the dark figures lurking a harmless distance away. The angel closest to Tom stood with shoulders back, chin lifted slightly, and his right hand resting comfortably on the hilt of his sword, a stance that sent a silent but clear warning of the consequences if approached. Human eyes could not see the angels nor could they hear the distant hissing as the rescue team moved Tom's broken body into the ambulance.

The angel next to Tom announced in a powerful voice clearly heard by the dark beings.

"Now is not the time. We will deal with you another day."

As the young paramedic secured the gurney into the ambulance rack, he noticed Tom's eyelids flutter.

"He's comin' around. Check the straps, I'll get us rolling!"

The ambulance pulled away, and its headlights passed across Big Mike's dust-covered empennage. The black tail numbers presented their final message as the light swept the tall vertical stabilizer: 5 – grace, 3 – resurrection, 7 – perfection, 8 – new beginning.

CHAPTER 42

David lay on a soft, warm surface, bathed in the scent of flowers and damp grass. He could see only white and felt incapable of speech. Moving his hands slightly, like a blind person exploring something new, he caressed the softness. As his hands moved, faint sounds floated toward him, seemingly created by his movements. Sounds that were familiar but mixed in a beautiful harmony with others he had never before heard. Sounds of a tinkling bell, small, faint, and beautiful—like tiny wind chimes in a gentle breeze.

Slowly, gently, the image of a face came into focus inches from his own, soft, smiling, and wonderfully familiar.

"Mom?" The sound of his own voice was unfamiliar to him.

"Yes," she whispered.

He managed to find a little more control over his new voice. "You look so young."

Then after a pause, she breathed. "Yes."

Her face glowed and smiled warmly as she looked down at him lying there on the grass. Then a tear of joy from her sparkling eyes fell onto his cheek. Her image faded as she stood. With her voice raised slightly, she called out, "Justice! He is here. Come and see, he is here."

Still reclined and looking up, David discovered his eyes were slowly adjusting to the soft light and brilliant colors of his immediate surroundings, but everything further than a few feet away was beyond his range of vision. He saw the blurry shapes of two images standing by him, one at his feet and the other, the taller one, standing at his side. The tall one bent down and extended a hand toward him. David reached up, gripped the hand, and felt himself effortlessly rise to stand.

As he rose, the face of the one whose hand he took came into focus. It was a face David remembered from the photograph of a young college graduate proudly holding his law degree. "Dad?"

He reached around David and placed his right hand on his shoulder. "Yes, I am here."

He looked toward David's mother. "Hope. Would you like to walk with us?"

"Yes, I would."

Although David recognized his parents, their names were new. On earth, his Dad's name was Samuel, or Judge Sam to most people. And his Mom was named Elizabeth but went by the nickname Liz. David would learn that everyone in heaven is given a new name—a name that fits God's call in his or her life and prepares each one for His purpose. With Justice on one side, his hand on David's shoulder, and Hope on the other, they walked across the soft grassy surface. After a few steps, Hope placed her hand in David's, entwining her fingers with his. No earthly words could express the peace, love, and correctness of the moment.

As they walked, David's sense of hearing continued to adapt to heaven's sounds. And although familiar, they were mixed with those completely new to him. Sounds in frequencies richer and sweeter than he had ever heard before. And the color-filled surroundings, although somewhat out of focus, had the same characteristic of familiarity blended with those he has never seen. Everything seemed to emit sound. The rocks under his feet snapped and popped musically. The grass made tinkling sounds like bells, and the trees swaying in the breeze reverberated in cords like harps and stringed instruments. The peaceful harmony and blending of the sounds flowed through the air everywhere, beautifully natural and alive.

Although he still felt dreamlike, David was adjusting to the reality that he was actually in heaven. He was also beginning to remember the angelic battle, the singing swords, and the angel that touched him.

"Dad ... Justice, angels fought for me. I remember three angels I think."

They stopped on a grassy hillside overlooking a meadow.

"Those are angelic warriors sent to bring you home. Sometimes just two or three and other times fifteen or twenty."

"Fifteen or twenty?"

Justice nodded his head.

"Yes. God and His angels know what battles they face and how much resistance there will be for every believer. New or fallen believers usually have demonic strongholds surrounding them. But God never loses one of His own. The angels see to that."

David was about to ask another question when suddenly a child ran by clutching a flower with brilliant blue petals and an intensely green-colored stem. The child tumbled down the hill, giggled, and jumped to his feet and then rushed off, continuing his adventure. Somewhere in the playful roll down the hill, he dropped the flower on the grass a few yards from David's feet. David watched the child disappear into a group of nearby trees and then noticed the discarded flower. He was about to look away when he saw it begin to move. And then, before his disbelieving eyes, it rotated in an aching movement and stood erect, petals facing the sky.

"Did you see that?"

Hope answered, "There is no death here. Not even the flowers."

Still thinking about the angelic warriors, he asked, "What about the children? How do they get here?"

Hope responded and Justice nodded in agreement.

"They just arrive. Their innocence and closeness to God protects them from every evil. There are no strongholds in them. They just arrive."

Justice held out his hand to Hope and then looked to David. "You will learn much of life and God, as you are ready. Come and see what He has prepared for you."

The horizon seemed endless, with beautiful rolling hills, meadows, streams, and majestic forests. As they strolled slowly down a gentle slope, David stopped and pointed to a nearby grassy hillside. "I know this place."

"Yes, we knew you would," Justice responded.

David slowly shook his head from side to side and began to laugh. Louder and louder until finally, looking at Hope and Justice, he pointed again at the hill.

"Jesus and I were there. I thought it was a dream, but look. See those two imprints in the grass. Jesus and I were there!"

Justice nodded. "Yes, and when you are ready, He will meet you there again."

Like a child standing in the middle of a perfect playground and just as easily distracted by all the choices and questions, David turned to Justice. "Are you shorter?"

After a short pause, Justice beamed a smile. "Remember? You always wanted to be six feet tall."

CHAPTER 43

"Continental Six Six … contact Las Vegas Approach on one two five point zero two five … good day."

In response to the radio call the co-pilot quickly pressed the yoke-mounted mic button and repeated the instructions.

"Las Vegas Approach on one two five point zero two five … Continental Six Six."

He reached to the center console and tapped a button on the computer to confirm the new frequency was correctly entered into Com 1. Then, after a pause to let a United Airlines flight on the same frequency finish a transmission, he jumped on.

"Las Vegas Approach … Continental Six Six … one five thousand … with information Victor."

He hoped the by-the-book radio work had been noticed.

"Captain Rawlins, I'd like to take it into Vegas?"

Chet did a quick scan of the instruments and turned toward the young man.

"We've got a full load. It's gonna be bumpy on descent, and there may be wind shear on final. You sure?"

Without hesitation, the co-pilot answered, "Yeah, I'm sure. I really want to do this."

Chet sighed deeply and moved his shoulders in a rotating motion. It had been a long flight and although he could not put his finger on it, something felt wrong and heavy on his heart.

He scanned the instrument panel one last time and nodded his approval.

"Your airplane. I'll handle the radios."

He cleared his throat, reached up, and switched on the cabin public address system. "Ladies and gentlemen, this is your captain. We're about to start our descent into Las Vegas. We've been advised that it's gonna be a little bumpy, so please stow your personal belongings and secure your tray tables at this time. We anticipate an on-time arrival. Thank you for choosing Continental Airlines. Flight attendants, secure the cabin."

Just as he finished the cabin announcement, the cockpit radio came alive.

"Continental Six Six … contact Las Vegas Tower on one one niner point niner."

Chet read back the instructions and quickly punched up the new frequency. "Las Vegas Tower … Continental Six Six … one five thousand."

The hurried voice of a busy air traffic controller responded, "Continental Six Six left turn heading one five zero … descend to six thousand … expect Runway Two Five Left."

The co-pilot followed the instructions, and the big 757 began its descent, banking south and turning away from the glow of the setting sun that was disappearing behind the Red Rock Mountains. With the co-pilot at the controls, Chet scanned the sky, looking for other traffic and noticed a dust cloud near the airport.

"Looks like we've got some dust devils south of the airport. Be prepared for a bumpy downwind."

Before the co-pilot could respond, the tower came over the radio. "Continental Six Six turn left heading zero seven zero … descend to four thousand to join downwind for Two Five Left."

As the plane settled onto the downwind leg, it passed the area where Chet had seen what he thought were dust devils. Instead, he saw an illuminated construction site filled with fire trucks, ambulances, and construction equipment surrounding what appeared to be a cabin-class twin partially buried in the dirt. He looked toward the co-pilot for a moment and then turned back to the window. "Looks like somebody lost it on departure. God, I hate to see that."

As politely as he could, the co-pilot asked, "You believe in God, Captain Rawlins?"

His gaze remained fixed out the side window as he pondered a response to the question. "I don't know."

The question and the unexplained heaviness on his heart brought painful memories of standing next to his Momma and watching Daddy's red Freightliner disappear in a cloud of dust.

"My problem is, when bad things happen to good people, where's God in that?"

Then after a short pause he continued. "A friend of mine calls Him the Hound of Heaven, but I don't know."

CHAPTER 44

The passengers were still getting their carry-on baggage from the overhead bins when Chet left the cockpit and headed up the gangway. The heaviness he felt had grown to urgency as the scene of the plane crash played in his mind like a looping video.

He dodged and weaved through the crowded terminal at a brisk pace with his black leather flight bag hanging from his right hand. Most of the adults who saw him coming stepped aside either out of respect for his uniform or submission to the determined look on his face. Normally, he would have noticed the little red-headed girl holding her daddy's hand, pointing and giggling as he rushed past. And normally the clanging sounds of the slot machines scattered around the terminal would have irritated him. But not this time. This time, he was aware only of the urgency to find out about the plane crash.

He arrived at the operations center, burst through the door, and rushed to the nearest desk. The young man at the desk leaned back in his chair as though bracing for impact as Chet stopped, dropped his flight bag onto the floor, and firmly placed both hands the desktop. He was short of breath as he addressed the clerk.

"Son, I need to know if you have any information about the plane that crashed."

Chet's uniform and demeanor had caused the other employees to stop what they were doing and watch as the young clerk gestured toward a chair next to the desk.

"Sir, I will be glad to help you. Would you like to have a seat?"

"No, I'm fine standing, and I apologize for bustin' in on ya like that."

The clerk immediately noticed the name tag on Chet's uniform jacket and the insignias indicating his rank.

"No problem, Captain Rawlins. I am aware of the incident. Let me see what we have in the file."

As the young man turned toward his computer monitor, Chet sat down in the wooden chair next to the desk and pushed his flight bag aside with his foot.

"Yes, Captain Rawlins, we do have some preliminary information on the twin that crashed tonight."

"What can you tell me?"

"Well, sir, to begin with, it wasn't a charter operation. It was a private aircraft registered to a San Diego business."

"Tail number?"

"November Five Three Seven Eight Mike."

The words hit Chet like a punch to the chest.

Seven Eight Mike ... NO!

He cleared his throat, attempting to speak, but could not. The clerk did not look up from the computer console as he continued. "There were two on board."

Finally able to speak, Chet asked, "Were there survivors?"

"It says here that both were taken to the trauma center at University Medical Center, UMC."

Somewhat relieved but still not believing what was happening, he hurriedly asked a last question. "UMC, where is that located?"

The clerk heard the urgency in Chet's voice and quickly responded, "1800 West Charleston. Good luck, sir."

Chet stood, picked up his flight bag, and then looked the clerk directly in the eyes. "Thanks for your help, son."

Chet spun toward the door and headed through the crowded terminal toward the taxicab loading area. At the curb outside the terminal, more than thirty people were waiting in the taxicab loading line. But three limousines were parked across the driveway, each with a driver waiting by the car. Chet walked briskly across the four-lane roadway, holding his left hand up toward the oncoming traffic. As he approached the long, black Lincoln parked at the front of the line, he called out to the driver, "Can you get me to University Medical Center on Charleston?"

The driver had watched the tall red-headed airline pilot march through traffic toward him and was reaching to open the passenger door before he had even heard the request. "Yes, sir, I certainly can."

CHAPTER 45

The crash site was cordoned off with orange police tape stretched from each of the four yellow portable light carts, creating a square field around the partially buried hulk. The wind caused the tape to flutter, and the flood lights reflecting off the trembling tape created random linear flashes like lasers through smoke.

Big Mike lay partially buried in the center of the site, with workmen under the fuselage removing dirt and debris with shovels and buckets. A large orange construction crane, with its lights shining on the pilot's side of the airplane, waited to lift the wreckage onto a flatbed trailer parked nearby. The gaping hole, where the pilot's side window and seat had been, created the illusion that a missile brought the airplane down. The crane operator shouted over the droning noise of the portable lighting units and the deep rumble of the crane's diesel engine.

"Good enough. Pull the slings through and get the rings on the hook. I'll take it from there."

Then he called out to the NTSB investigator.

"Mac, we need to pop the wings before I can trailer it. You want to do anything before we break it down?"

Mac had worked his way up from the San Diego FAA field office and was now an investigator for the NTSB. Coincidentally, he was in Las Vegas attending a joint NTSB/FAA seminar on airport security when he received a call regarding the crash. He did not know that the pilot in command of the wrecked airplane had worked for him at one time—nor would he have cared. A high-profile investigation in a major city would look good in his personnel file and to him, that was all that mattered. He just happened to be in the right place at the right time. It always seemed to work that way.

He held his hands up to the crane operator as a stop signal and shouted back.

"Yeah, let me get more photos. And before you get it on the trailer, I need to tag the parts. You know the drill."

The big hook on the end of the crane's cable was poised several feet above the wreckage. The large metal rings that hung from the hook were connected to wide, dirty yellow straps that cradled the fuselage at two locations, one just behind the wings and the other next to the hole where the rescue team had pulled the Tom and David from the wreckage. The crane operator shut down the crane and climbed out of the cab.

One of Mac's two subordinates walked toward him with a black leather briefcase in hand.

"Found this strapped in one of the seats. Looks important."

Mac reached out and took it by the handle.

"I'll take it from here. Now go police the area for parts that may have left the airplane. And find that missing fuel tank. Collect and tag anything metal. I don't care if it looks like part of the plane or not, I want it!"

The two men walked away with flashlights in hand. One turned to the other, shook his head, and grumbled. "Jerk!"

Mac heard but ignored the complaining subordinate. He was more interested in the expensive briefcase hanging in his right hand. He noticed the tumblers on the right lock were set at 993. Out of curiosity, he set the third tumbler to 9 and tried the lock. Nothing. After looking around to confirm that no one was watching, he tossed the briefcase into the open window of his black Ford Taurus rental car and walked to a nearby pickup truck where an open toolbox sat on the bed. He found a large common screwdriver and walked back to his car with the tool held to the side of his leg like a gunman holding a six-shooter in his holster. He pulled the briefcase back out of the car and set it down on the hood, unknowingly upside down. It was then that he noticed the tumblers on the left latch read 666. The unusual finding inspired him to set the right tumblers to 999. Both latches popped open.

CHAPTER 46

The telephone rang again, but Margie was afraid to pick it up. It was almost certainly news she did not want to hear.

The caller a few hours earlier had been evasive about Tom's condition except to say that he was at the Las Vegas UMC Trauma Center being stabilized for surgery. They had not said anything about Mr. Adams, and Margie had been too shocked to think of asking. She had arranged to have a close friend come by and get the twins and was sitting home alone, worrying and afraid to answer the telephone. Jenny had also called and, although distraught, she had offered to arrange Margie's transportation to Las Vegas.

On the fifth ring, Margie mustered the courage to answer and spoke in a cautious whisper. "Hello."

"Mrs. Winslow, this is Chet Rawlins. Do you remember me?"

Margie did not immediately recognize the Southern drawl, but the authority in his voice gave her a faint feeling of protection and safety—two things she lost when she answered the midnight telephone call from hospital. Then she remembered. "Oh, Chet, yes, I remember." She paused and took a deep breath. "Do you know about …"

Before she could finish, Chet interrupted. "Yes, I do. I'm on my way to the hospital. Is there anyone there with you?"

"No. I'm just waiting."

She paused again then continued. "I'm waiting for Mr. Adams's office to call me about how to get to Las Vegas."

"I can get you here." Chet said with stern confidence.

"Oh, but what about ..."

Chet apologetically interrupted again. "I'll take care of everything. Can you be ready to go in two hours?"

"Yes, I'm ready now."

Then, softening his voice and speaking more slowly, Chet continued his instructions. "Someone from Continental Airlines will call for your address and pick you up. Just go with them and I'll meet you at the airport here in Vegas. Understand?"

For the first time since the horrific telephone call, Margie's mind and heart felt a hint of relief and hope. The power and confidence of Chet's voice caused her to sigh deeply. "Oh, thank you so much. I didn't know where to begin. I just want to be with him so badly, and the hospital wouldn't tell me anything about him or Mr. Adams."

Her voice trailed off into sobs, allowing Chet to patiently continue his instructions. "You'll be picked up and taken to the airport. They'll drive you directly to the next Continental flight heading to Vegas. You won't go to the terminal. They will take you right to the airplane."

"Oh my. And how do I pay for my ticket?"

"You don't. You just go with them and I'll pick you up. Understand?" Then, before she could answer, he continued. "We're pullin' up to the hospital now. I'll see you soon."

Before she hung up, Margie asked, "Will you call me after you see him? I need to know how bad it is."

Chet wished this was not happening, and he definitely did not want to become the messenger of bad news. "I'm sure they're OK. They're both a couple tough cowboys. I'll see you soon."

Within fifteen minutes of the call from Chet, the telephone rang again.

"Mrs. Winslow, this is Continental Airlines. Captain Rawlins has instructed us to transport you to Las Vegas. May we have your address and the nearest cross street so that our shuttle can pick you up?"

CHAPTER 47

The new hospital was in operation, but it was obvious the project was not completely finished. The palm trees that would eventually grace the entry driveway were still in boxes; the back parking lot was graded gravel; and the contractor's construction trailer could be seen near the rear of the unfinished parking area.

Chet's limousine pulled into the driveway where a sign indicated trauma center. Dust and the scents of mulch and fertilizer were carried in the night breeze as the limousine slowed to a stop next to the large glass doors of the trauma center lobby. Chet opened the door, grabbed his flight bag, and walked briskly toward the doors before the driver could perform the customary duty of opening the door for his passenger.

Chet had already paid for the ride and waved over his shoulder to the limousine driver.

"Thanks, friend."

The driver looked at the crisp one hundred dollar bill in his hand, smiled, and shouted back, "Thank you, sir."

The pretty young blond sitting behind the built-in reception desk looked up when she heard the glass doors automatically hiss open. Then, in response to seeing the tall uniformed airline pilot walking into the lobby, she pulled her shoulders back and sat more erect in her chair. The moment she and Chet made eye contact, she cocked her head to one side and smiled flirtatiously. "May I help you, sir?"

Chet looked around the empty lobby before answering, "Yeah. There were two men brought here tonight. They had been in an airplane crash. Thomas Winslow and David Adams."

She studied the information on the computer monitor for a moment. "Yes, sir. Mr. Winslow is in the trauma center, and Mr. Adams, let's see, I don't see him here. Oh."

Her flirtatious smile and sexually teasing body language suddenly stopped, and she made every effort to avoid eye contact with him. "Just a moment, please."

She pressed an illuminated blue button on the reception desk telephone control panel, and within seconds they were joined by a stocky, middle-aged woman with a butch haircut and wearing a masculine-cut gray business suit, including pants and a tie. The receptionist handed her a yellow index card. She glanced at the card and then held her hand out toward a room just off the lobby, inviting Chet to join her there. He followed her toward the room and, as she held the door open for him to enter, he noticed the word "Chapel" engraved on the diffused glass.

Without speaking, the woman sat down in one of the four chairs that surrounded a low, round, highly polished black marble table. Chet sat in the chair directly across and waited.

After a short pause, she looked at him and asked, "Are you related to Mr. Adams or Mr. Winslow?"

In his already-heavy heart, he sensed where the conversation was going, and the added emotional weight caused him to slouch down in the leather chair. Then he looked down at his hands as though the answer was written there. "No. Just a very close friend."

She nodded her head and continued in a tone of voice that sounded very much like an interrogation. "Are you helping the families in any way?"

Chet finally looked up from his hands and took a deep breath. "Yes. I have arranged to have Tom's wife brought here. But really,

I don't know if Dave has family. He and I are close friends, that's all."

As he spoke the words, he sensed that he probably should have said "were close friends."

The woman reached out and placed her left hand on Chet's clenched fist in a feminine gesture that belied her appearance and demeanor. "What is your name?"

"Chet, Chet Rawlins."

Although she did not say it, her brother was an airline captain, and she recognized the insignias on Chet's uniform. "Captain Rawlins, your friend Mr. Winslow is in very serious condition and in surgery as we speak. His survival is going to depend on his health before the accident and his will to live."

Chet leaned forward, rested his elbows on his knees, and placed his hands over his mouth. "And Dave, Mr. Adams?"

For a moment, she did not answer but instead peered into Chet eyes, as if looking through him to the wall beyond. Then she leaned back in her chair and raised her hands in a surrendering gesture. "I'm sorry, Captain Rawlins, but Mr. Adams did not survive the crash. They brought him here shortly after Mr. Winslow arrived, but he had already passed. There was nothing we could do. I'm very sorry."

Before he could respond, she said, "I'll leave you now, but I'll be near the reception desk if you need me."

Chet sat with his head down and his eyes fixed on the surface of the black marble table and mumbled, "Thanks."

The anger growing inside him began to overpower the denial that had sustained him. And although he did not have a clear memory of how he learned to express anger, he slammed his fist down onto the table and spit the same foul words that blasted from his Daddy's mouth the day he backed the box trailer into the shed. Then, almost as quickly as the anger had come upon him, guilt took its place. His mind filled with thoughts, questions, and condemnation.

Why did this happen? What were they doin' flying to Vegas? I should have called them before I did. I thought Tom stayed in Phoenix. I could have done something. Hell no, I should have done something!

Almost a half hour passed before Chet emerged from the chapel. His eyes were red and his vision blurred by tears as he slipped past the reception desk and through the lobby doors. The dry, cool night greeted him with a puff of earth-scented air as he stood looking up at the star-filled sky.

"By God, I'll find out what really happened, and I will protect Tom and Margie from this mess."

He flipped open his cell phone and hit redial. "Hello?"

"Margie, this is Chet."

She nervously interrupted. "Oh, Chet. I talked to the airline, and they are on the way to get me. Thank you." Then after a short pause she continued. "How is he?"

"Tom's in surgery, and they haven't told me much yet. By the time you get here, we should know more."

In answering, he intentionally avoided the seriousness of Tom's condition and the passing of David Adams.

"Margie, do you know where Tom keeps his log books?"

Although not sure why he was asking, she did not question his motive. "Yes, he keeps them in the drawer of his nightstand."

"Could you please bring them with you? I'll explain more when you get here."

"I'll call you when I get there."

"There's no need to call me, Margie. I already know your flight and arrival time. I'll be there to pick you up."

Margie interrupted before Chet could finish. "Oh, the shuttle is here. I've got to go now."

As Margie boarded the shuttle in San Diego, Chet flagged a taxicab waiting near the hospital entrance and gave instructions to the driver.

"Take me out to a construction site near the intersection of Las Vegas Boulevard and Blue Diamond Road. I'll tell you when we're close."

CHAPTER 48

The cab pulled over and stopped on the gravel apron of southbound Las Vegas Boulevard just past Blue Diamond Road. Chet climbed out and leaned into the open passenger window.

"Wait here."

The gravel surface changed into rock-strewn sand as he neared the new temporary chain-link fence surrounding the crash site. Signs were fastened to the fencing at ten-foot intervals: "No Trespassing by Order of the National Transportation Safety Board."

Beyond the fence, he could see a large area where desert plants were crushed in a maze of tire tracks. The tracks surrounded a long trench that began at an earthen mound and tapered off to the north. The full moon cast long shadows over the ground and into the long, dark trench. It was widest at the earthen mound and continued to the right, ending in the shape of a point, like the tip of a freshly sharpened pencil, pointing, aiming directly toward a place three miles away that Chet knew was the departure end of Runway One Nine Right.

It was unimaginable to him that Tom could have done anything to cause this disaster. Something must have failed or gone horribly wrong. And why didn't he try to make an emergency landing at Henderson Airport just a few miles to the southeast? Something outside Tom's control must have happened. All of those questions begged answers. Answers that would result in bureaucratic and insurance nightmares for Tom and Margie. And if he carried out his plan, the nightmare would include him.

The dim glow of sunrise shown beyond the barren mountains to the southeast. As he walked back to the waiting cab, his eyes stayed fixed on the ragged outline of the Providence Mountains.

CHAPTER 49

Consciousness came slowly with a merciful lapse back into sleep. The images in his mind were a jumbled mass of those he last remembered. They came in a smattering of disjointed, still visions, like photographs spilled from a shoebox. The quick flashes in the slideshow appeared and then were blinked away, only to be replaced by another before the previous image could be fully understood. He saw a quick image of the earth coming up to meet an airplane and, for some reason, his view was from the cockpit. And then in a flash he saw a man in the seat next to him. David, David Adams. Dave.

The image of David's lifeless body strapped into the co-pilot's seat with his head tilted back was the key that Tom's mind needed to unlock the events he struggled to remember. With the memories came the smell of dust and fuel and the taste of blood along with the distant sounds of banging, shouting, and the involuntary moan that emitted from his throat just before he fell into the deep pool of blood-soaked unconsciousness.

The sounds and images in his mind competed with the noises and light that surrounded his hospital bed. His head and body ached in spasms of intense, throbbing pain as he slowly awakened. In his mind, he saw a bright rainbow ring that grew larger and closer with each painful breath until it passed by him, showering prismatic light across his closed eyes. Then slowly, cautiously, he opened them and squinted against the ache that radiated around his head. Ghostlike and blurry images stood next to his bed and through the pain he heard a familiar soft voice.

"Tommy … honey … Tommy. Can you hear me?"

He parted his lips and wetted them with his tongue in an attempt to respond but could not. The pain that surged through his body and head blocked any hope of an audible response. Chet rushed out of the room and found a nurse sitting behind the counter of the nurse's station.

"Excuse me. The patient in Room 107 is …"

Before he could finish, she jumped to her feet and walked briskly toward the room, signaling to a nearby doctor. They entered the room, and the doctor bent down, holding his face a few inches away from Tom's.

"Mr. Winslow, can you hear me?"

As the doctor waited for a response, he held open Tom's eyelids and moved a small flashlight beam back and forth over his pupils.

"Looks like he's with us."

CHAPTER 50

Not all of the signage had been installed in the new building, only those critical to the hospital staff and fire department. "Cafeteria" had not made the critical list, and it took some hallway searching for Chet and Margie to find it. Margie sat at a glossy gray laminated table while Chet looked for the coffee bar. He quickly returned carrying two white mugs of steaming coffee and sat across the table across from her.

"Careful, it's hot."

Before she could respond, he asked the question that had motivated him into action since leaving the crash site a few hours earlier.

"Did you bring Tom's log books?"

Margie reached into her brown leather oversized handbag, pulled out a large white envelope, and pushed it across the table toward Chet.

"They are all here. Can you tell me why they're important? Did Tommy do something wrong?"

Chet opened the envelope, slipped the six black log books onto the table, and answered without opening them. "No, Margie, Tom didn't do anything wrong. These books are only important to people who want to find a way to blame him for the crash. They call it 'pilot error'."

"Why would they do that?" she asked with a childlike, puzzled look on her face.

He pulled the books closer to himself. "Bureaucracy. Margie, I need to keep these. If anyone asks you for them, tell the truth. You gave them to me. That's all you know. I asked for them, and you gave them to me. Understand?"

Before she could answer, they were interrupted by the same nurse who had sent them out of Tom's room twenty minutes earlier.

"You can see him now, but please be careful. He shouldn't move."

Margie quickly stood and asked, "Can he talk? Is he coherent?"

The nurse's tone of voice became like that of a teacher addressing problem students.

"He can see you and hear you but," she paused for effect and continued. "It will be difficult for him to speak. The doctor has been communicating with him by limiting the questions to yes and no and watching his fingers."

"His fingers?" Margie asked.

"Yes. The doctor has told him to raise his index finger for no and two fingers for yes. But really it would be best if you just sat with him and limited the stress of communicating. In a few days, he will be in much less pain and more coherent."

She nodded in response to the instructions and then followed the nurse toward Tom's room with Chet close behind. He held the valuable envelope close to his side, gripping it as though it were bundles of hundred bills. Margie's mind was swimming with needs and hopes as she prepared to reunite with the physically broken man she loved. She needed to understand the severity of his injuries, and she hoped that somehow she could speak without breaking down.

Chet waited outside the room for a few minutes, giving Margie time to find her emotional footing and reconnect with

Tom. He leaned on the wall just outside the hospital room door, completely unaware of the activity in the busy hallway. He had finally accepted the reality of the crisis and now understood that it was not his fault and that there was nothing he could have done to avoid it. Having thought through the possible ramifications of his plan, Chet nodded his head and said softly aloud, "Now it's time for action. It's time."

He tapped on the door and then slowly opened it a few inches without looking in. "Can I come in?"

"Oh, Chet. Yes, come in. He seems to fade in and out. I guess it's the drugs. Oh God, I'm so glad he's alive. He smiled at me with his eyes."

With those words, she began to cry and backed away from the bed where she dropped onto nearby chair, dabbing her eyes with the tissues wadded in her hand. Both of Tom's legs were in encased a fiberglass cast from his hips to his toes, and a cable system connected the cast to weights suspended from a chrome frame at the foot of the bed. Another cast surrounded both of his shoulders and extended down his left arm, leaving only his fingers and thumb exposed.

His right arm was bandaged at the wrist, and a small clear tube ran from an IV stuck into his forearm to a clear pouch of fluid suspended from a chrome bracket at the head of the bed. Although the dressing wrapped around his head covered his temples and his ears, his face was exposed except for the bandages applied to his left cheek and jaw. Kneeling down at the side of the bed. Chet spoke softly.

"Tommy, it's Chet. Can you hear me?"

He watched Tom's fingers, extending from the cast, and saw his index and middle finger slowly rising, creating a trembling V.

The relief Chet felt was involuntarily expressed by a deep sigh and tears that he tried to squint away. He took another deep breath and prepared himself to ask Tom for permission to act on the plan. The tears pooled on his lower eyelids, and he wiped them away with the sleeve of his wrinkled uniform jacket. He leaned closer to Tom's right ear and whispered.

"Tom, I have your log books."

Then, empowered by the innate fight-or-flight instinct that boiled within him, he asked the question: "Should I burn them?"

There was no response for several seconds as Chet looked intently into his eyes and then, without moving his head, Tom slowly looked down toward his left hand. Chet's eyes followed, and he saw Tom's fingers extended from the cast in a rigid, shaking V.

"Done!" Chet exclaimed.

He wanted to reach out and grasp Tom's arm or somehow make a physical connection with him to affirm their bond in this heroic decision, but Chet resisted. He turned slowly toward Margie and stood, extending his six-foot-two-inch frame to full height with his shoulders back, as though at attention.

"I'll be in the lobby. I'll wait for you there."

Then with the envelope containing Tom's log books securely held at his side, Chet left the room, his thoughts locked on the next step of the plan: the mountains south of Las Vegas.

CHAPTER 51

The dark maroon Ford Expedition rental rolled down Interstate 15 heading south, its headlights piercing the night with Chet slouched in the driver's seat. Cruise control held the lumbering SUV at seventy-five miles per hour as he pondered the events that had crashed into his life over the past thirty six hours.

He had left Margie at the Hampton Inn, located just within walking distance of the hospital. And although it was against airline policy, he used the Continental Airlines credit card to secure two rooms for a one-week stay. He had finally gotten out of his wrinkled uniform and, after a quick shower, changed into his favorite civilian clothes: blue jeans, a long-sleeve white shirt, boots, and a baseball cap.

As he drove hypnotically to a vaguely determined destination, his thoughts wandered back to the simple days of Momma, Daddy, and the dusty little farm house on the side of a Texas gravel road. The big rigs traveling south with him raised memories of Daddy and the big red Freightliner. Then the familiar haunting question that lurked deep in his wounded heart moved in and surrounded the images in his mind.

Why do bad things happen to good people?

And, as usual, no answer.

He passed long rows of trucks and RVs as they began to struggle up the interstate's steep climb just south of Prim, Nevada.

The sound of his own voice caused him to sit erect and place both hands on the steering wheel.

"Where in the hell am I?"

Then he reached over the center console and patted the envelope resting on the passenger's seat. An approaching freeway sign indicated an exit ahead, and Chet noticed a smaller brown sign just beyond it.

Mojave National Preserve, Next Exit.

Obeying what he believed was a spontaneous decision, he took the exit onto the rolling two-lane road and continued several miles east until he saw another brown road sign.

Providence Mountain Campgrounds.

He slowed down, found the turnoff, and turned right off the asphalt roadway, causing the SUV to kick up rocks and dust as it skidded slightly onto the graded dirt. The road beyond his headlights was faintly illuminated by a waning moon and stars that covered the clear night sky, drawing him further and further away from Las Vegas and its painful worldly realities.

Everything he thought was secure and everything he believed was safe had been shaken and ripped away. He had lost one of his closest friends. The other was lying in the hospital, shattered and held together with pins and casts. And he was about to destroy evidence related to a federal investigation.

An all-too-familiar question passed through his mind. *Where's God in this?*

Unaware of the spiritual forces that led him deeper into the isolation of the mountains, he continued along the washboard road until he came upon another brown sign, soot-covered and partially charred.

Campground, 2.0 Miles.

He turned onto the narrow two-track trail just past the tilted sign. Burnt pine trees and the twisted remains of junipers stood along each side of the trail, evidence of the Hackberry Fire that raged through the campground years earlier. Ahead, illuminated by the headlights, he spotted the remains of several campsites with parking areas and fire rings.

He pulled up to the first campsite and stepped onto the graveled surface. A cloud of fine dust and ash rose and settled onto his boots with each step. There was no one around, and there were no sounds except for the crunching of the dusty gravel as he walked to the rear of the SUV. The unique, simple sound of gravel under boots brought sad memories of Daddy coming home, Momma's cooking, Goldie, and the carefree, innocent life he once knew.

He opened the big hatch and pulled out a bag of matchless charcoal briquettes. After a pause to bathe in the memories that seemed more real than the air he breathed, he tossed the bag into the fire ring. Dust floated into the air. He struck a match from the book of paper matches he found at the hotel. It took only a few seconds for the briquettes to ignite, creating a halo–like glow around the fire ring and illuminating Chet's somber face. The heat warmed his hands as he squatted down and gently placed the first log book onto the heap of glowing coals.

"Oh God, oh God. I'm so sorry, Tom, but we gotta do this."

Those words and the grief welling up inside caused tears to flow and spill onto the dusty ground as he continued the painful task of destroying the written history of his friend's life as a pilot. Each page curled as if trying to escape the inferno that relentlessly grew stronger, consuming everything it touched.

"Hell. I'm living in hell."

After placing the last log book into the fire, he walked a few steps back to the SUV and sat on the dusty ground, leaning against the bumper facing the hungry blaze. Sitting there, emotionally exhausted and feeling the weight of a world collapsing around him, he stared at the fire, determined to stay until every page was destroyed. Then, with a matting of moist dirt, ashes, and tears near his eyes, he looked up to the star-filled heavens.

"God, where are you in this? I gotta know!"

At first, there was only silence. Then, in the distance, he heard the low, mournful howl of a dog or a coyote. He stood to his feet, looked toward the direction of the sound, and cried out.

"Hound of Heaven? Is that you?"

Hearing nothing, he shook his head and angrily responded to his own hopeful question. "I didn't think so!"

As the last of the log books faded into ashes, he looked up with his face toward the soft cool breeze to see a shooting star rip across the sky from east to west. Frozen there for a moment, he wondered about the coincidence of the star. And just as he was about to move, another distant howl was carried to him by the wind.

CHAPTER 52

David's briefcase sat on the floor next to Mac's feet. In it were three cell phones and seven manila folders. It was the manila folders and some surfing on the Internet that prompted Mac's visit to the Department of Homeland Security, or DHS. That and a possible shot at a promotion from the NTSB to the DHS.

He was early for the appointment and as he waited, he placed the briefcase on his lap and pulled it open. The manila folders inside were organized alphabetically in the file holder of the briefcase lid. Each folder contained 18- by 24-inch structural drawings folded in half. The drawings illustrated an area of reinforced concrete and included a group of reference notes. Although none of the information indicated the location of the buildings for which they were intended, the title blocks on the lower right corner of the sheets included what appeared to be a coded name. A different name for each drawing but not really a name, just three capital letters. It was the three-letter coded names on the drawings and some surfing of the Internet that taunted him.

Each of the three letter names coincidentally matched the FAA designations for seven western airports. In preparation for the meeting, he had looked them up in a pilot's guide and scribbled notes next to each title:

ABQ = Albuquerque Int'l, NM (Civilian and Military)

CHD = Chandler Muni, AZ (Civilian near Sky Harbor Int'l)

GYR = Goodyear, AZ (Civilian near Luke Air Force Base)

LAS = Las Vegas International, NV (Civilian near Nellis Air Force Base)

OGD = Ogden Hinckley, UT (Civilian near Hill Air Force Base)

PSP = Palm Springs Int'l, CA (Civilian near 29 Palms Military Base)

TUS = Tucson Int'l, AZ (Civilian and Military)

The other clue that the briefcase was likely part of some devious plan was the combination for the locks. Everybody knew that 666 was supposed to be a code for the Antichrist, the Devil. Mac did not believe there was a devil or a god. Still, the numbers haunted him.

On the night before the meeting, he surfed the Internet for the number 666 and found a huge list of sites, some just weird and others more informational. He clicked on a site titled Biblical Numerology and discovered that not only was 666 supposed to be a code for the Devil, but the number 6 was the code number for man. Something about being created on the sixth day.

The site was easy to operate and seemed to produce answers that confirmed his suspicions. So he typed in 999 and discovered that it was code for the last days of the earth, the Tribulation. It became obvious to him that the dead guy in the plane crash was part of some fanatical religious group planning to terrorize America. He was sure the information sitting on his lap would spur a federal investigation. And he intended to lead it. Self-righteous anger welled up inside him.

Muslim terrorists! Christian fanatics! If it wasn't for religions, none of this would be happening!

He made a vow that he would expose and destroy anything to do with religion, especially Christians and Jews. It was their fault. The Muslims hated them and so did he.

CIRCA AD 2012

CHAPTER 53

More than a year had passed since David's funeral, yet the fight raged on. Accusations of fault and demands for money blasted among insurance companies, lawyers, bankers, and bureaucrats. All equally guilty of greed, they postured and accused, twisting the truth in their battle for maximum financial benefit. With words and paper as weapons of choice, a seemingly endless flow of letters, reports, affidavits, and disclaimers shot between the warring parties, all for the purpose of dodging responsibility or to fill financial coffers.

Fortunately, David had covered Big Mike with adequate insurance for the battle. However, unexpected challenges posed by the lawyers representing the contractor of the damaged construction site added yet more confusion to the mêlée. The construction site where Big Mike crashed had been fenced off, and no work was permitted until the court could determine that all possible evidence had been gathered and all parties had been allowed to perform their investigations.

Like sharks following blood through water, the contractor's lawyers saw the disaster as an opportunity to demand policy limits from David's insurance company. The legal documents they filed claimed property damage, delay damages, and stigma. In truth, the contractor was over budget and behind schedule, which motivated his lawyers to go after all of the insurance money. The whole pot. More than enough to bail the contractor out of his financial mess while earning a substantial fee for the law firm. And if others depleted the insurance, David Adams's corporate holdings would be their next target.

As for Chet, Continental Airlines had placed him on indefinite furlough with half pay pending the results of an internal investigation into misuse of company funds and benefits. Although his misuse of the company credit card to obtain lodging and provide meals for Margie was at issue, it seemed that Chet's orders to have her transported pro bono from San Diego to Las Vegas had created more administrative grief than anyone could have imagined.

A flight attendant on the Boeing 737 that brought Margie to Las Vegas had asked to see her photo identification. After confirming that Margie was not a member of Captain Rawlins's immediate family, she saw an opportunity to get back at the airline pilots who had sexually harassed her over the years and didn't care that Chet had not been one of the offenders.

As she discovered, calls to the DHS were processed quickly and, best of all, with anonymity. For her, the chaos and the administrative grief inflicted on the company and its pilots pacified her anger while keeping her role in the alleged security problem invisible.

There was also the matter of an ongoing investigation regarding information contained within the NTSB accident report alleging Chet's involvement with the destruction of pertinent case evidence. The report included the following paragraph:

The wife of the pilot in command, Mrs. Margaret Winslow, testified that Captain Chester H. Rawlins had taken possession of the accident pilot's log books. Furthermore, when interviewed by the NTSB, Captain Rawlins confessed, without hesitation, to having destroyed them.

No criminal charges had been filed, but Chet was being watched closely by the airlines, the NTSB, and the DHS. His employment records with Continental, and his log books had been subpoenaed and therefore had become public records that revealed flight instruction hours with David.

Tom was home in San Diego and, although healing fast, he remained confined to a wheelchair. Unfortunately, even if he mended completely, his flying future was at risk. The FAA withheld his pilot's license pending completion of the NTSB investigation report, which included the following summary:

Without further evidence to the contrary, our preliminary investigation findings include pilot error, which contributed significantly to the accident. The findings are based on the pilot's failure to properly preflight the airplane, remove contaminants from the fuel tanks, return to the airport of departure or divert to nearby Henderson Airport, and failure to maintain control of the airplane, resulting collision with terrain.

As part of the post-crash investigation, the NTSB had dismantled the engines, examined the fuel tanks, inspected the plane's airframe, and dug through Big Mike's maintenance log books. The conclusion was that all systems were functioning at the time of the accident and that the right engine had failed due to water contamination in the fuel.

With exception to an easy round of depositions, Tom and Chet had been miraculously spared from the string of hearings, expert depositions, and conferences that filled the court's calendar. But then they received calls from David Adams's lawyer requesting their attendance in a meeting at his office, one described as urgent and extremely important.

As Chet pulled into the driveway, he saw Tom push open the front door and approach the car with Margie guiding his wheelchair. Chet was the first to speak.

"Morning, Tom."

Tom's casts had been removed, but he was not allowed to put weight on his legs without using crutches because of the pins in his ankles. With Margie's help, Tom climbed into the passenger seat.

"Got your phone message. I can't believe they pulled your pilot's license."

Before Chet could answer, Margie reached over Tom's lap, snapped his seatbelt, and kissed him on the cheek.

"Go get 'em tiger," she said with a giggle and then closed the car door, stepped back, and blew him a kiss.

Tom smiled warmly at her and then turned back to Chet.

Chet looked out the rear window, put his right arm on the back of the seat, and began backing out of the driveway. "It's worse than that, Tom." He paused, and took a deep breath. "Continental fired me."

"My God! FAA took you're license, and Continental fired you?" Tom exclaimed. "What are going to do now?"

Chet kept his eyes on the road ahead and answered, "Not sure. Maybe I'll start drivin' trucks again."

The two men rode in silence.

CHAPTER 54

The long conference room with its massive bookcase-covered walls engorged with law books and dark mahogany furnishings created a distinctly authoritative architectural statement that was made even more intimidating by three large portraits of the law firm's original, though now-deceased, partners.

Tom and Chet sat alone at the highly polished conference table, Chet in one of the sixteen dark brown leather chairs and Tom next to him in the wheelchair. The receptionist had escorted them to the conference room and then returned with coffee in dainty clear crystal cups on equally delicate matching saucers, which seemed out of character when compared to the room's dark masculine atmosphere.

Chet was about to comment on the fragile cup he held carefully in one hand and the delicate saucer he held in the other when the door opened. Two men wearing expensive, dark, pinstripe business suits entered the room. One was carrying a cardboard document box and the other held a cordovan leather briefcase in his right hand. The lawyer, the first to enter, set the document box on the nearby credenza and walked to the head of the table.

"Good morning, gentlemen, good to see you. I believe you both know Mr. Adams's accountant and financial advisor, Mr. Solman."

Matthew Solman nodded as he approached the conference table. He sat his cordovan briefcase on the table but remained standing.

"Good morning, Tom."

"Morning, Mr. Solman."

Then he looked toward Chet. "Mr. Rawlins, I believe we met briefly at the memorial service. Mr. Adams spoke highly of you, and as I recall he had offered you a position with his company but you went into the airlines instead. And gentlemen, please call me Matt. We need not be so formal."

Matt's offer to drop the formalities did not relieve Chet's discomfort. The location of the meeting and the interrogational feel of the conversation prompted him to simply respond, "I remember you from the funeral, but other than that I don't think we've met."

The attorney remained behind the chair at the head of the table, and Matt stood behind a chair at the opposite end. The arrangement placed Tom and Chet in positions similar to spectators at a tennis match, requiring them to look left and right as the drama continued. Matt walked over to the credenza, opened the box labeled "Trust of Seven," removed several large yellow envelopes, and sat them on the table near the attorney. He then pulled a letter-sized white envelope from the box and returned to his seat.

Tom and Chet watched in silence, still unsure about the purpose of the meeting and both suspecting their lives were about to be radically changed.

After a few more seconds of ominous silence, seconds that felt like minutes, Matt took his seat. As he did, the attorney who remained standing opened one of the large envelopes and removed a spiral-bound letter-sized document. He placed it unopened on the table and began.

"Gentlemen, as Mr. Adams's attorney, I represent his trust. As such, I have called this meeting for the purpose of determining the future status of the trust. Information will be discussed this morning that is highly confidential, and we would ask that you understand and acknowledge the importance of that confidentially. Furthermore, if after our initial presentation you feel the meeting should not go forward, please tell us. Do you understand?"

Tom and Chet exchanged glances and Tom spoke first. "I understand. Please continue."

Chet's discomfort caused him to intentionally delay. And when he finally did, the response was mumbled. "Yeah, I understand."

Then he looked down at his hands, waiting and assuming that this meeting was going to screw up his life even more.

The attorney sensed Chet's discomfort and subtly changed his demeanor, softening his body language. As he did, the tension in the room lessened. It was a trick he used in jury trials, and it usually worked. In a friendlier tone of voice and with a warm smile, he nodded to Matt. "Matt, you're up."

Matt pushed back his chair and stood but did not look up at the men. Instead, he kept his gaze fixed firmly on the white envelope that lay on table before him.

"Tom, Chet, Mr. Adams has no family. I don't know whether you knew that or not."

After a short pause, he looked up at them. His eyes squinted slightly as though what he was about to say was very serious or even painful.

"We have a letter here that Mr. Adams had instructed be read to both of you. But before we open the envelope, I want to remind you again of the confidentiality of this meeting and the information you are about to be given."

Both Chet and Tom sat with their eyes fixed on the mysterious envelope and then nodded in acknowledgment without speaking. Matt's presentation permitted Chet to feel somewhat more relaxed, in great part because the man was not an attorney. Matt looked toward the attorney and, after seeing him nod in agreement, continued with the presentation.

"Good. Then let me proceed with reading the letter."

Slowly and ceremoniously, he slipped a polished mahogany letter opener across the top of the white envelope. He removed the folded one-page letter and placed it on the table. He sat down, rested his forearms on the table edge, and gently grasped the letter, holding it delicately in both hands as if it would break if dropped. He looked up at the men and then back down at the letter and began reading.

"PERSONAL AND CONFIDENTIAL

"To Thomas Lincoln Winslow and Chester Hamilton Rawlins, my close and trusted friends.

"This letter is being read to you because I am either incapacitated or no longer alive. However, as you both know in your hearts, my absence does not mean that I am dead. No, rather I am fully alive with my Father in heaven and hope to see you here someday. While on earth, I prayed that the Hound of Heaven would seek you out, and I stand in faith believing that we will meet again. But until then, God has important work to be done.

"I have established a Trust for the purpose of helping believers survive the time of tribulation that is coming. In the trust, I have included the requirement that there never be less than two nor more than three trustees. As I am no longer there, I have instructed my attorney and my fellow trustee, Matthew Solman, to ask you to prayerfully consider joining the trust. I believe in my heart that God will lead you to know His will for your lives and for His use of this trust.

"Alive in Him, David."

The silence that filled the room amplified the sounds of deep breathing and the shallow sighs emitting from the men. The attorney and Matt understood that if Tom or Chet did not accept the position of trustee, they would be required to terminate the trust, thereby dissolving all financial and liability protection of assets and throwing open the doors to liquidation and taxation. Tom and Chet felt the weight of the major decision that was now on them. Tom broke the silence and asked the first question.

"How much time do we have?"

The attorney answered, "We are technically out of time, but if we act this week, I can make it work. I don't know if you men realize how this affects Mr. Adams's corporation and the lawsuits caused by the plane crash. Matt, could you explain?"

Tom felt the sting of fault and anger touched off by the words of the attorney. And as he relived the painful memory of the crash, a reoccurring question returned to haunt him.

How could water have caused the engine failure? I bled the tanks! There has to be something else, there has to be!

Unfortunately, neither Tom nor Chet would ever know. As sometimes happens in life, random changes to parallel circumstances prevent any hope of reconnecting the dots that once provided a path toward truth. And when it happens, the facts are separated, never to be connected again. A separation as far apart as east is from west.

On the morning following the crash, the new fuel trucks arrived at the airport, purged, filled, and immediately placed on the line. The old truck that had been used to fuel Big Mike was hauled off to an auction yard somewhere in Arizona. Two days later, the lineman filed for divorce and quit his job at the airport. He had no idea that his failure to bleed the fuel/water separator had ultimately caused the engine to fail.

Tom's introspection was interrupted when Matt responded to the attorney's request.

"Yes, the airplane crash and its related legal problems will be compounded by loss of the trust. You see, David's corporation effectively has no assets other than insurance monies, the crashed airplane, office equipment, and his Mercedes. All other assets he has acquired are held in the trust and as such are not owned by the corporation or exposed to corporate liability."

The silent pause that followed Matt's words grew until it owned the room. For Chet, it seemed impossible that he could help in the legal and financial matters of a trust. Matters that were important to David, even in death. The death of a really good man. Where could God be in that?

Tom, however, knew in his heart that he had been prepared for the task. As he silently remembered his encounter with God, his hand slowly turned the saucer under his coffee cup. Light rays from somewhere in the room passed through the crystal and emitted a small curved line of prismatic colors that danced on the polished surface of the conference table near his hand. The sight caused him to gasp, swallowing the memory of the rainbow ring and David's childlike excitement. No one in the room was aware of the divine guidance flooding over him as God used the power of the incredible memory and the miracle of his own survival to fill him with confidence, resolve, and urgency. His voice pierced the silence. "Then it's obvious what we've got to do. I'm familiar with trusts, Matt, and I'm willing to come on board with you."

Then he turned his wheelchair toward Chet. "What about it? You up for it?"

Chet, who had been looking down at his hands and avoiding eye contact during most of the verbal exchange, took a deep breath, looked at Tom, and answered, "I'm no good with money. I can't do this."

The shock and disappointment of Chet's words caused Tom to lean back in his wheelchair and glare at him in disbelief. "Chet, this is important. You've got to!"

"Nope. Can't do it."

And with that statement, he pushed back his chair, stood, and walked toward the door. "I'll wait for you in the car."

Tom's determination to save David's trust overpowered everything he cared about, including his friendship with Chet and his disappointing decision. "No. You go on. I'll call Margie."

The lawyer, accustomed as he was to drama, quickly joined the exchange. "I'll see you out, Mr. Rawlins."

Tom took a deep breath as if to purge away the conflict and turned to the only other person left in the room.

CHAPTER 55

For Chet, the elevator ride down to street level symbolized the sinking feeling and unbridled hopelessness that hung on him. The door hissed open, and he walked through the white marble floor lobby toward the tall glass wall that faced the street. A beggar sitting on the sidewalk just outside the exit doors looked up to Chet as he slowly walked by.

"God bless you. Got any spare change?"

Chet pulled a twenty-dollar bill from the pocket of his starched white shirt and set it on the beggar's outstretched hand.

He looked at the bill and then up to Chet. "Bless you, man. God bless you!"

Blessings from God were the furthest thing from Chet's mind. The depth of his sadness spoke for him. "Blessed? Hardly."

Chet turned south and walked along the curb, avoiding eye contact with the people passing him, some nodding, some smiling. He could not understand why. Amid the din of bus and traffic noise, a dog barked, a sound seemingly out of place in the busy city streets. He looked in the direction of the bark in time to see a new white Chevy Tahoe pass by with a yellow Labrador sticking his head out the passenger window. His ears and floppy lips were blown back by the wind, mimicking a toothy smile.

As he watched the Chevy roll by, memories of Goldie riding in the back of Daddy's pickup floated to the surface, briefly casting light into his dark depression. Then the bumper sticker on the Chevy's back window caught his eye: JESUS LOVES YOU.

He shook his head, looked down at his feet, and continued toward the parking structure. Across the street, the bells of an old greystone church began to chime. Next to the church steps stood a straggly line of homeless men and women, dirty and dressed in tattered, discarded clothes. At the top of the steps, a young minister in a long black robe and white collar greeted each one, inviting them in for a hot meal. Chet could faintly hear the minister's warm voice as he placed his hand on the drooping shoulder of a homeless man.

"God bless you, sir. Welcome to God's house."

Chet's sadness deepened.

CHAPTER 56

"OK, Matt, where do we go from here?"

"Tom, I'm very pleased that you agreed to this important task, and I'm sorry about Mr. Rawlins's decision."

The frustration caused by Chet's decision sounded in Tom's succinct response. "Me, too. Where do we go from here?"

The intensity and resolve expressed by Tom's words, made even more obvious by his stern facial expression, prompted Matt into action. He set his briefcase on the table and slowly positioned the briefcase lock tumblers: 666 on the left and 999 on the right. The latches popped open, and he lifted out a laptop computer and a compact projector. He placed them onto the conference table, connected the computer to the projector, and plugged them into the power receptacle partially hidden in the center of the table. Then, without speaking, he stood and walked to the cabinet on the only portion of wall not covered with bookcases and portraits. Opening it, he exposed a built-in projector screen.

"Let me tell you more about the trust, the rest of the story, so to speak."

Tom sat silently and mentally braced for the impact the presentation could have on his life.

"First and foremost, let me remind you that the information we are sharing is to be held in close confidence and only between the two of us for now. Unfortunately, I must ask you not to share the details of the information, even with your wife. There will come a time when others can be included but not yet."

Tom nodded in affirmation and watched as the image projected on the screen brightened into focus.

The Trust of Seven/Summary of Holdings.

Matt continued. "This information exists on the hard drive of this computer and on one backup disk. Unfortunately, portions of the information were also in David's briefcase, which, as you may know, is in the hands of the federal authorities."

After a quick sip from his water glass, he continued. "David had a very successful and lucrative architectural practice. However, what you may not know is that he also accumulated a substantial number of income properties and a collection of investment portfolios with various brokerage houses. The bottom line, Tom, is that David reinvested every dollar of profit from the trust held properties and a great deal of the income from his practice."

Matt then tapped the computer's touch pad and the next page appeared on the screen.

Real Property/Property Income/Schedule of Investments/Net Worth.

"This is a list of the assets held in the trust. As you can see, we are responsible for projects in a five state area: Arizona, California, Nevada, New Mexico, and Utah. Most are condominium units, approximately four hundred in all, but there is also a concrete tilt-up warehouse in Nevada and the office building here in San Diego."

He paused, cleared his throat, and continued by tapping the computer touch pad again. Rows of numeric columns with subtotals and totals filled the screen. Matt aimed a laser pointer at the figure on the bottom of the page. "This, Tom, is the net worth of all the properties, bank accounts, and investment portfolios as of yesterday."

Matt gave him time to review the information and intended to guide him through the document, but before he could, Tom spoke out in a startled, childlike voice. "Two hundred and twenty million dollars!"

Matt smiled and nodded before abruptly changing the subject. "Tom, can you travel?"

"Yeah. I'm supposed to use crutches for a while, but I can travel."

Matt smiled warmly. "So then you aren't confined to the wheelchair."

"No, I just do it to keep my wife and the doctors happy. I get around fine, a little stiff, but I can deal with it. Why?"

Matt looked at his briefcase and then back at Tom. "I need to show you something, but it may be too strenuous for you. Could you handle a trip to New Mexico?"

Tom chuckled and cocked his head. "No problem."

Matt leaned closer to Tom. "Are you familiar with the Scriptures regarding healing?"

Tom looked puzzled. "Healing? No, not really. David talked about it once in a while, but no, not really."

Matt pulled a worn black leather-bound Bible from his briefcase and opened it. "Tom, there are hundreds of promises in here about God's love for us and His desire that we be whole spiritually and physically. Can I pray for you?"

Tom leaned closer to Matt and nodded but did not speak. Matt stood and moved behind him, placing his hands on Tom's bent shoulders. "Father, thank You for Tom. Thank You for his survival in the crash. Together we stand on the promises of Your Word, and we ask that any remaining damage to Tom's body be healed. We love You, Lord. Thank You for the amazing love You have for us, Your children. We praise You and, in the name of

Your Son Jesus, we believe that Tom is healed and whole in body and spirit. Amen."

Before Matt had finished praying, Tom felt a warm sensation begin at the soles of his feet and intensify as it moved up his legs. When it passed his ankles, where the pins had been placed, it increased in intensity until he was sure that hot coals were touching his skin. When Matt finished praying, Tom moved his feet off the wheelchair supports and stood. As he did, the heat faded away and so did the pain. He turned to Matt.

"My God!"

Matt smiled and nodded. "Yes. God."

CHAPTER 57

Raindrops splattered onto the surface of the swimming pool and along the barbeque deck and the palm tree fronds waved rhythmically as the wind increased. Tom gazed out the window as he sat at the desk of his home office. He was on the telephone with Chet, their first conversation since the trust meeting at the attorney's office.

"Tom, please don't try and convince me to get involved. I just want to get my life back."

Tom took a deep breath before responding, "I know. That's not why I called."

Before Chet could respond, he quickly continued. "I need you to listen to what I have to say. When David and I made our last flight, something happened that changed my life. David lived a life that can only be described as miraculous. And the way he was able to do the things he did was because of his relationship with God."

Chet mumbled something, but Tom did not stop. "He gave his life to Jesus. And Chet, I gave my life to Jesus too. He loves you and if you just let Him, He will fix everything."

There was a pause before Chet responded. "I know, Tom, but I'm just not ready. My flyin' is done. I'll be OK. I just need to get my life back together."

Tom attempted to speak, but Chet continued. "Let me work it out, Tom. Maybe someday I can go there. But not right now."

And with that, he hung up. Tom set the handset back onto the telephone and stared out the window. The rainfall was heavier. He was about to pray for Chet when Margie knocked on the door.

"Tommy, I need to talk to you."

The oppressive spirit that had filled the room was moving through the house. He stood, pushed the chair back under the desk, and followed her to the living room. She curled up on the couch with her feet tucked under a pillow, and Tom sat on the overstuffed chair next to the couch.

"Tommy, I need to know what's going on."

He leaned forward and looked deeply into her eyes. "I'm sorry, honey, I can't tell you yet. But believe me, it's something I must do."

"But I don't understand. You go off to a meeting that you said was important and then you come home, pushing your own wheelchair, and won't tell me what it was about.

Tom attempted to speak, but she continued. "And then you plan to fly off somewhere. I need to know what's going on. I don't like it! I don't like it at all!"

The last time he felt so powerless was when Chet walked out on him at the trust meeting.

"I love you, baby."

His voice softened to a gentle whisper. "I really love you, and I really need you to understand. Soon, I don't know when, but soon, I can tell you what God is doing for us."

Graciously, the doorbell rang. Matt stood at the door under a black umbrella. He sensed the stress as Tom swung the door open.

"Good morning, Tom. Good morning, Mrs. Winslow."

CHAPTER 58

The commercial flight to Albuquerque was an opportunity for Matt to continue briefing Tom on the work of the trust. They sat in a row of three seats with an empty seat between them. On the empty seat lay the briefcase Matt had brought along to help Tom grasp the plan and intent of the trust.

"There are seven special condominium projects under construction for the trust, each with a hidden underground chamber. Three in Arizona, one in California, one in Nevada, one in New Mexico, and one in Utah. Today we're going to see the one in New Mexico."

Tom wanted to respond but was as speechless as the day he awoke in the Las Vegas hospital following the crash. He was stunned by the amazing secret that his departed friend had kept from him. A Scripture David often quoted floated through his mind.

Romans 8:28: And we know that in all things God works for the good of those who love him, who have been called according to his purpose.

Matt placed the briefcase on Tom's lap. "This is yours. In it are duplicates of everything in David's briefcase."

Tom scanned the black leather and silver trim and then placed his hands palm down on the lid, like a pianist preparing to play. Matt continued. "You'll find envelopes labeled with three letter tabs. The envelopes contain everything you need to know about each location. Notice that the letters match various airport identifications. That's because the projects are located within radio receiver range of nearby airports. It will help the Select hear what is happening above ground and, more importantly, know when it's safe to come out of hiding."

Tom nodded and asked, "Select?"

"Yes. God will select those for whom the chambers have been prepared. He will call them, and He will guide us on the timing. For now, we're to continue the preparation and soon, very soon I think, we'll begin to hear from them."

He paused as a flight attendant walked by and then leaned close to Tom's ear.

"The combinations for the briefcase are 666 on the left and 999 on the right."

Tom dialed in the combinations and opened the case.

"Each of the twelve projects has sealed chambers below ground equipped for shelter and survival. The chambers are located below the second level of the underground parking garages. Sealed inside are crates packed with medical supplies, dried food, military surplus ready-to-eat meals, bedding, books, puzzles, exercise equipment, batteries, flashlights, and almost everything imaginable for a long stay."

Matt was interrupted by an announcement from the cockpit.

"Ladies and gentlemen, we are beginning our descent into Albuquerque. Flight attendants, prepare the cabin for landing."

Tom closed the briefcase, snapped the latches, and spun the locks. He turned toward Matt and asked, "You married?"

Matt smiled and nodded .

"Yes. And we have two children, a boy, seven, and a girl, five. How about you?"

"Yeah, twins. A boy and a girl. You could probably tell Margie wasn't happy about me taking this trip. But to tell the truth, what she's really mad about is not telling her what you and I are up to."

Matt nodded sympathetically. "I understand. My wife is very displeased about my work with the trust. But unfortunately we can't tell them what's going on. Not yet."

CHAPTER 59

Chet stood facing the red behemoth with his hands stuffed in the front pockets of his blue jeans and a folded cashier's check in the pocket of his starched white shirt. The salesman put on a toothy smiled as he approached.

"What do yah think? Got some miles on her, but she's not near ready for the boneyard. She's a Freightliner."

Of all the used trucks scattered around the lot, it seemed right. It was the only Freightliner with less than five hundred thousand miles on the odometer and the only tractor with a seventy-inch sleeper. And it was red. The Arizona summer breeze warmed Chet's face as he turned toward the salesman. He slid his hand across the freshly polished left front fender and gave the tire a tap with the toe of his boot. The salesman responded to the symbolic tire kick with a nod and a question. "You drove her. What do you think? Worth thirty-four nine?"

Chet looked down at his hands and then reached up and patted his shirt pocket containing the folded cashier's check. "Throw on some new tires, and I'll give you thirty-three out the door."

"Ouch. Let's go inside and see what my manager says."

Chet was ready for the cat-and-mouse game of used equipment dealers. Cars, trucks, airplanes; it did not matter. The game was the same. They entered through the glass door into the cool air of the small sales office. The salesman handed Chet a copy of the truck's specification sheet and offered him a seat at his desk.

"Take a look at the specs, and I'll pass your offer by the boss."

With that he walked toward the nearby cubical of the sales manager. Chet looked over the one-page document:

2006 Freightliner; Odometer 423,000; Sleeper 70" RR; Engine Detroit 14.0L 435; Engine Brakes; FA Capacity 12,000 lbs; RA Capacity 40,000 lbs; Suspension Air Ride; 5th Wheel Airslide; Power Steering; A/C; Cruise Control; Tank Capacity 130 gal.

He tossed the sheet onto the desk and picked up a copy of *Flying J Long Haul* magazine. As he thumbed through the pages, the memories came. Memories of Daddy with his feet up on the coffee table flipping through the pages of the *Long Haul*. Memories that were warm and relaxing, carrying with them sounds and scents: the sound of Daddy's deep voice, the scent of apple pie, and the warmth of Momma's hugs. He hoped that buying the truck would get him the peace he struggled to find. The sad reality that he could not go back to those days caused him to lower his head and sigh. He looked up as the salesman approached.

"Mr. Rawlins, here's what we can do." He set a sales contract on the desk and waited for Chet's response.

"I said thirty-three thousand out the door, and that's what I meant."

The salesman leaned forward and whispered, "Look, Chet. Mind if I call you Chet?" Then he continued before Chet could respond. "I really need to sell you this truck. If I don't sell a truck today, I'm in big trouble with the boss."

Chet unfolded the cashier's check, laid it down on the table facing the salesman, leaned across the edge of the desk, and looked him squarely in the eyes. "I understand. Believe me, I do understand. But I've got this much to spend. How about just new front tires?"

He raised one eyebrow and reached for the check. "Mind if I borrow this for a minute?"

Chet knew the sight of cash and a commission would prompt the next move. "Go ahead. We make a deal and it's yours."

The salesman picked up the check and walked away briskly, like a kid leaving a candy store with a fistful of goodies. Chet stood and walked to the full-height window next to the glass door. There, across the lot, stood the red Freightliner, waiting, ready to take him to a new future. He chuckled as a Willie Nelson song began to play in his mind.

On the road again, just can't wait to get on the ...

"Chet, come on back to the desk and let's do this deal."

He turned and walked toward the smiling salesman.

"We can put front tires on the rig and let her go for thirty-three five, tax and license. Out the door like you want. Can we sell you this truck today?"

CHAPTER 60

Cliff picked up Matt and Tom at the airport in his white Ford 350 crew cab pickup. It was Sunday afternoon and traffic through town was light.

Tom had chosen to sit in the back seat, while Matt sat in front with Cliff. Matt had not been to the project and was eager to see the surroundings and proximity to the airport. Tom leaned back against the headrest and watched the familiar scenery flow by. The images brought memories of his trips to Albuquerque with David.

Cliff pulled up to the project's security gate and tapped in the key code. The construction trailer had been hauled off, the desert landscaping finished, and, except for the "No Trespassing" signs, it looked normal and ready for occupancy. Only Cliff, Matt, and Tom knew of the chamber and only Cliff knew how to access it.

The gate swung open and automatically closed behind them. Cliff pulled up next to the garage entrance and parked his truck parallel to the opening, blocking both access and view into the garage.

"OK, fellas, we're here. How do ya want to do this?"

Matt answered, "Just show us around, Cliff. We'll ask questions as they come up."

Tom nodded in agreement.

Cliff climbed out of the truck first, glanced around the empty project, and then signaled for Tom and Matt to follow. They walked down the ramp and felt the air temperature grow cooler as they descended. It carried with it a scent of damp concrete and fresh paint.

As their eyes adjusted to the dim natural lighting, Tom noticed the only two objects in the garage. Cliff walked directly to the one on the right. The size and apparent purpose of the machinery became evident as they approached. Although it appeared to be a garage ventilator with louvered fans built into the walls and ductwork extending from the top to the outside wall, they would soon see that it was much more.

Cliff pointed his flashlight beam down to the lower right corner of the machine. There, a bead of weld in the shape of a cross about one inch long had been burned onto the frame. However, unlike the traditional Christian cross, it lay horizontal. Cliff explained, "It was my idea and David OK'd it. First I did it to bless the chamber, but when I went to do the weld, I realized that it needed to be there so as to show which of the air handlers was the right one and which panel to pull."

He handed the flashlight to Tom and glanced back at the entrance ramp to assure no one was around. With a quick yank, he pulled open the louvered panel next to the cross. It was hinged at the top and as he held it up, Matt and Tom stooped and peered inside. Cliff handed Tom the flashlight.

"Climb in. I'll tell ya what to do once you're in."

Tom knelt down and crawled through the square thirty-inch opening. Inside, he discovered a metal hatch built into the floor.

"Do ya see the hatch on the floor?"

"Yeah."

"Okay. Now shine the light around the walls in there. When you do, you'll see a couple radio antennas and some twelve-inch ductwork that's goose-necked down at the top. See it?"

"Yeah."

Cliff turned to Matt and said, "When you get in there do the same. I'll tell ya what they're for when we get inside."

Matt nodded in response.

Cliff continued his instructions. "Tom. Now I need you to scoot back away from the hatch and look for a D-ring hooked to a cable on the side wall. When you find it, pull it. But watch out when you do, cuz the hatch is gonna swing down."

Tom shined the flashlight beam along the metal wall and spotted the D-ring. Once sure that all his body parts were clear, he pulled. He heard a click under the floor and the hatch swung away.

BANG! CLANG!

Cliff leaned toward Matt's ear. "I oughta put some padding on that I guess."

Matt did not respond. Instead, he was beginning to wonder if he and David had made the right decision in hiring him.

Cliff continued his instructions. "OK, Tom. Now I need you to climb in the hole. Look for a steel ladder bolted to the wall in there and then leave the flashlight on the floor next to the hatch. Go down far enough for Matt to get on the ladder too."

As Tom felt his way down into the dark chamber, the air became cooler and the scent of damp concrete and fresh paint intensified. It was too dark to see the floor below, and the sensation of being suspended above a bottomless pit caused him to tighten his grip on the ladder. Matt crawled into the air handler and then cautiously climbed down the ladder until just his shoulders were above the hatch opening. Then Cliff slipped into the air handler and pulled the louvered panel closed, locking it with two levers mounted inside the frame.

"Now that I pulled these levers down, we're locked in. The same thing works on the floor hatch. It's locked from inside the chamber. And now I can tell you about the stuff here inside.

The radio antennas are connected to a coaxial cable that runs down into the chamber where battery-powered radio receivers are gonna be connected. Tom, can you hear me?"

Tom's voice echoed in the darkness. "Yes."

"The duct with the goose neck has been run down in the chamber and is hooked up to an air filter system. It's made to keep radioactive and biological warfare stuff from gettin' in. That'll keep fresh air comin'."

Tom called up from the darkness. "Can we continue this down here?"

Cliff leaned over Matt's shoulder and apologized into the darkness. "Sorry, Tom."

He handed Matt the flashlight.

"Flashlight's comin', Tom. Go ahead and climb on down."

The men gathered at the base on the ladder, and Cliff reached to a nearby electrical switch surface mounted on the concrete block wall. He clicked it up and the wall next to them illuminated. The pools of light washing the wall revealed the overall volume of the chamber, an area the size of two side-by-side tennis courts and a ten-foot ceiling. Several large wooden crates stood in the center of the space. Other than the crates, the LED light fixtures and the air filtering system, the place looked empty.

"The lights are runnin' off the storage batteries over there."

Cliff pointed to a corner of the chamber where a collection of marine deep cycle batteries were lined up on a three-tiered shelf system. Next to the batteries were boxes labeled "bikes and alternators."

"Those boxes have exercise bikes and car alternators that need to be put together. The instructions and tools are in the boxes. Once they're built, they'll be hooked up to the batteries. As long as somebody's pedalin', the batteries get charged."

Tom asked, "Why are the lights on the wall?"

"Oh, those. They're gonna simulate days. The lights are on a timer that's set to different parts of a day. Since it's near dinnertime, it turned on the west wall. East wall is morning, ceiling is daytime, and, like I said, west wall is evening. He had me paint the east wall light green, the ceiling light blue, and the west wall light orange. Said the colors and lighting would help 'em keep track of the days."

As Cliff continued explaining the layout and systems of the chamber, Tom felt the sensation of claustrophobia creeping over him. Much like the helplessness of being encased in a body cast and connected to a hospital bed like a cable-bound puppet. To shake it off, he asked a question that had been nagging him since entering the chamber.

"What about water and sewage?"

Cliff smiled and then answered, "Water was the tricky part. We had to punch the well after the chamber was sealed off. Took some doin', but we got down far enough to get water, about four hundred feet. It's a small pipe, but with that twelve-volt pump over there, she flows pretty good."

Tom shook his head side to side and asked.

"How on the world did you get down four hundred feet without a drilling rig?"

"Wasn't easy. Once we got the concrete cored, we attached a jig around the hole and set up an electric drill and a bit with diamond teeth on six-foot pipe sections. Took a Honda gas generator up in the garage to run the drill. That was the part that had me worried most. I was sure somebody'd hear the generator and follow the power cord to the air handler, but they didn't."

He turned and pointed to the opposite corner of the chamber.

"Over there, about six feet up from the floor, is a big plastic tank. See it? Under there is a pipe that goes through the wall. All the sewage gets pumped up to the tank and then when you turn the valve, it runs out of the tank and into the gravel on the other side of the wall."

Matt looked puzzled and asked, "Won't it seep back through the wall and into the chamber?"

"Nope. We waterproofed the wall and backfilled it with enough gravel to handle it. I'm pretty sure it'll work."

———

The tour continued for another hour. By the end, both Matt and Tom were convinced of two things: One, the Select would be safe and healthy in the chambers. Two, Cliff had done an excellent job of following David's instructions.

As they drove back to the airport, Tom asked about the other six chambers.

"The crates for Arizona and Nevada are already in place and the chambers are set up. The rest are still in the Nevada warehouse and need to be shipped and set up," Cliff explained.

Tom turned to Matt. "I know who can help transport the crates when the time comes."

"Who do you have in mind?"

"Chet. He has experience with large trucks, and I'd like to keep him involved with us somehow."

Matt gazed out the window and tilted his head to one side. "Where is he spiritually?"

Tom shrugged his shoulders and answered, "I'm not sure. I'm just not sure."

Matt responded, "We'll see. How about we pray together before anything more is discussed."

Cliff asked, "Can I pull over and pray with you guys?"

Matt nodded. Cliff merged over, pulled into a wide area next to a call box, and stopped. The men locked hands, like a team in a huddle, and bowed their heads while Matt prayed.

"Father, thank You for all that You have done through David and for allowing us to continue the work. We have no agenda but to follow You. We ask for Your guidance and wisdom for every minute of our lives and in every decision we face. We understand and believe that You, the Great I Am, know all things and know the future before it happens here on earth. We ask that You show us what to do and when to do it in the hope that these preparations will benefit those You choose to call. Thank You, Father, for Tom and Cliff. Empower us and guide us with Your Holy Spirit. We ask these things in Jesus' name. Amen."

CIRCA AD 20??

CHAPTER 61

Three thousand two hundred eleven satellites orbited the Earth. Five hundred fifteen of them were dead, nothing but space junk. And the space junk count was on the rise. Something was causing healthy, functioning satellites to malfunction or shut down. Or worse, slip from their assigned orbits and crash to Earth.

The signals from GPS satellites were misplacing latitude and longitude positions by thousands of miles; communications satellites were pulsing barrages of static earthward; and spy satellites were sending erroneous images. The scientists at NASA and the National Oceanic and Atmospheric Administration, NOAA, frantically researched potential causes and attempted in vain to communicate with the ailing space-borne equipment.

It was their collective efforts to solve the satellite dilemma that revealed the horror. They had discovered three separate space-borne threats, not just for manmade satellites, but for the very survival of life on Earth. They knew that each threat carried an arsenal of potential destructive power far beyond man's ability to oppose. There was no defense. There was no shelter. And it appeared that there was no worldly hope.

The nearest threat was from the sun. Scientists had been monitoring solar flares for decades, and the data clearly showed an increase in activity over time. However, the frequency and the intensity of the activity had spiked exponentially. The X and M Class solar flares, with their accompanying solar wind and radiation, would not only disable satellites and cause radio blackouts; the long-lasting radiation storms would threaten the stability of the Earth's polar magnetic field.

The second threat was from an increase in gamma ray bursts coming from deep space. Gamma rays are emitted from supernova explosions and discharge more energy in ten seconds than the sun will release in its entire lifetime. The Earth's atmosphere had always absorbed gamma rays with little impact on mankind, but recent observations of several supernova explosions beyond the Milky Way indicated that a massive wave of radioactive atoms bombarding the Earth was imminent. Radioactive atoms that kill living cells.

The third space-borne threat was an object discovered when deep-space photographs from the Hubble Space Telescope were compared to the last round of images received. NASA immediately notified Washington, which in turn provided the findings and the locations to every country with a space observation program.

At the time of the discovery, the deadly asteroid appeared to be a mere stationary dot of light. But as the world's observatories and radio telescopes zeroed in on the location, they discovered that the light intensity was steadily increasing. As scientist compared data, it became clear that not only was its trajectory aimed directly at the Earth but its size eclipsed that of the 900-foot-long asteroid near the Earth called Apophis. The scientists agreed to name the new asteroid Omega.

Theories regarding the effects of the solar flares, speculation of when Omega would penetrate the Earth's atmosphere, and the potential destruction of it all blasted across the airways and the Internet like scorching heat from a nuclear shockwave.

The entire world was drawn into the crisis regardless of politics, religion, education, or status. Every nation with nuclear weapon capabilities went on high alert in anticipation of a possible attack from another country. World war gripped mankind like a hangman's noose and with it the inevitable doom of a fiery end to planet Earth. The news media called the worldwide, frantic human behavior "End Times Panic."

The only question remaining was which of the destroyers would deal the final blow: the asteroid, the gamma rays, the Sun, or a manmade nuclear holocaust.

CHAPTER 62

There were icy patches where the mountains shaded the road and loose gravel where rock slides scattered debris onto the pavement. Common road conditions for truckers making the Interstate 70 run from Denver to Los Angeles in the fall.

Chet's fifty-three-foot-long flatbed trailer was loaded to maximum weight with crushed scrap iron pressed into heavy cubes. The compressed masses had once been automobiles and household appliances but now were reduced to blocks of twisted metal, broken plastic, and shattered glass.

The air temperature was dropping as the sun touched the horizon. His visibility through the streaked windshield fell to almost zero when the big rig rounded the curves that turned him west. The speed limit for his gross weight was twenty miles per hour on the seven-percent grade down the west descent, 8.6 miles past the summit and the Eisenhower Tunnel. He used engine braking to ease the load on the air brakes, but the weight of the rig and the pull of gravity pushed the speedometer higher each time he eased off the pedal. This was the heaviest load he had hauled since buying the used rig.

The trailer brake imbalance had not shown itself until now. It was caused by sloppy repair work and prevented the brakes from slowing the wheels uniformly, causing some of the wheels to work harder than the others. When the loads were light, the defect slept. But when the loads were heavy and the brakes heated up, the imbalance caused the brakes to fade and the trailer to swing.

The only thing Chet could see clearly as he rolled around a westerly curve was the speedometer needle at thirty miles per hour and the trailer in the mirrors. He was a little too fast, and the trailer was beginning to swing toward the centerline. If he sped up to straighten the trailer, he might not make the curve. If he was heavy on the brakes, he could jackknife. He struggled with the deadly decision.

"No choice. Slow her down and hope she don't jackknife."

CHAPTER 63

Bits of concrete and fine dust fell from the ceiling, confirming that the jackhammers and heavy equipment were about to breach. The chamber's occupants—twenty-five men, twenty women, a pair of six-year-old twins, and two siblings under the age of twelve—huddled in prayer. Suddenly, the muffled pounding stopped.

"Hold it! I found something!"

The voice was from Mac, now a DHS agent. After discovering the contents of David's briefcase and completing the investigation of Big Mike's crash, he had successfully moved from the FAA to the DHS. His job was to investigate any and all threats to the airports included in the list found in David's briefcase.

The investigations in Utah were closing in on a condominium project east of Ogden Hinckley Airport, but work had to be stopped when the military evacuated a five hundred-mile area surrounding a secret nuclear missile site in the desert near Salt Lake City. The evacuation was triggered by the discovery of electronic malfunctions of the missile's arming and targeting computers. Malfunctions that could result in an unscheduled launch or a silo detonation.

Mac had moved his team to Arizona and zeroed in on a condominium project just south of the Tucson airport. His team was equipped with highly sensitive electronic equipment capable of pinpointing locations of functioning radio receivers. And although the building had been abandoned following the Oro Valley earthquake that ripped through Tucson, his equipment clearly indicated radio receiver activity in the rubble.

The workmen dropped their tools and gathered around a section of the collapsed wood-framed floor structure and a partially crushed garage ventilator that had been raised together by a forklift. The lifting of the ventilator had revealed an opening in the concrete floor that was thirty-two by thirty-two inches.

Mac cupped his hands together and shouted into the darkness, "Hello! Anyone in there?"

Silence.

"Bring me a ladder and a light."

As he knelt down to peer into the dim opening, a 350 millisecond burst of light flashed through the darkness. Had he blinked, he would have missed it. Immediately following the light, a soft sound drifted by, the sound of clothing falling to the floor. He did not hear the sound, but he did feel the cool breeze that flowed up from the chamber.

He crawled out from under the ventilator and marched toward the workmen, intending to scold them for not following his orders. When he found them, they were pointing toward the street where several cars and a bus had just left the roadway and plowed into buildings. One of the men called out, "Over there, man! What the hell!"

———

At that very moment in the Rocky Mountains, Chet was fighting a life-and-death battle to keep his big rig from sliding out of control into the canyon. He eased the big rig around the curve and glanced into the mirrors to check the trailer. To his surprise, another tractor pulling a box trailer came into view. It rolled closer to the left rear corner of his trailer and drifted across the centerline. That was when he saw it. There was no one in the cab.

He double clutched a downshift and pressed harder on the smoking brakes. As he steered around the curve, he watched helplessly as the unmanned truck tapped the side of his trailer. The force of the impact stopped the trailer swing, straightened the rig, and gave Chet just enough time to hit the accelerator as the curve became a long straightaway.

Unmanned cars and motor homes littered the road ahead and in the sky he could see jet contrails bending and turning in crazy patterns as if a dogfight was happening at high altitude.

The high-pitched whine, like a diving fighter jet, caused the workmen to turn and look into the sky over the airport. They watched helplessly as a commercial airliner screamed straight down toward the Earth, instantly vanishing in a huge cloud of dust and smoke. The sound of the impact followed two seconds later.

Mac turned to the group of men and discovered that where one of them had been kneeling beside a truck, only his clothes and boots remained. The men panicked, jumped into their vehicles, and raced out of the project, leaving Mac standing alone, shrouded in dust.

The military had been on high alert, with thousands of aircraft filling the sky since the End Times Panic began. Air traffic controllers were overburdened, and the inevitable occurred directly over the spot where Mac was standing. A Tomcat fighter jet and an Apache Gunship, both fully armed, slammed together a thousand feet above him. The explosion and shockwave from the midair collision caused him to duck and look up. The twisted metallic remains of the two aircraft, some of it aflame, scattered over the construction site in earth-shaking thuds. He watched in helpless horror as death approached.

The impacts shook the concrete garage structure, imploding the walls and causing the weakened ceiling to collapse into the chamber. But the occupants were not there. Every chamber was empty of occupants. Every child and Christian, living and asleep, everywhere in the world, had been taken away in the blink of an eye.

———

Chet pulled the big rig off the road and stopped near a small sedan where a woman was kneeling beside the open rear door. Groups of people were huddled next to vehicles, some weeping and others standing on the edge of the roadway staring at the sky. As he climbed down from the cab, the woman who had been kneeling by her car came running toward him pointing back at the car and the empty car seat.

"My baby! My baby!"

EPILOGUE

The sudden disappearance of men, women, and children of all ages from every part of the old Earth marked the final leap in humanity's flight to the Promise. A promise of warning to all and hope for those who believe in Jesus. A promise recorded and preserved in the Bible for all who chose to listen.

"For in the days before the flood, people were eating and drinking, marrying and giving in marriage, up to the day Noah entered the ark; and they knew nothing about what would happen until the flood came and took them all away. That is how it will be at the coming of the Son of Man. Two men will be in the field; one will be taken and the other left. Two women will be grinding with a hand mill; one will be taken and the other left." Matthew 24:38–41

For those who turned away, there was only one choice: perish in the chaotic fiery demise of the old Earth. But for those who accepted Jesus as Lord and Savior, the end of life on the old Earth marked the first day of life on the new Earth. A new and perfect world where there is no death, no suffering, and the only tears that flow are tears of joy.

"Do not let your hearts be troubled. Trust in God; trust also in me. In my Father's house are many rooms; if it were not so, I would have told you. I am going there to prepare a place for you. And if I go and prepare a place for you, I will come back and take you to be with me that you also may be where I am." John 14:1–3

AFTERWORD

Books and movies, with mystery and adventure, where heroes do battle for good over evil. Such are the make-believe worlds we are drawn to, often as an escape from perceived realities. And in the escape, we hope for distraction from the burdens that feel too heavy or the monotony that creeps into our lives. Having been created with an innate drive to survive and an involuntary fight-or-flight instinct our "flight" often takes us to the fictional salve of manmade entertainment. But the temporary relief is just that … temporary.

The permanent answer, the eternal answer, to life is here now and only a heartbeat away. He came to the earth as the child of a virgin, the one the angels called "God with us." He is Jesus, the promised Savior. He teaches with allegorical stories and real-world miracles. He gives eternal answers to life's temporal questions. And for those who answer His call, He overcomes the burdens, tedium, and anger that darken mankind's short time on earth.

Let me encourage you. Let me challenge you. Within you lies the amazing story of your life used by God. Fight your way through the doubts and lies and let your flight be to Him. Find Him, follow Him, and stand in faith, sure of what you hope for and certain of what you do not see. It is my prayer that this book lifts you high, where the view is clear and the true story of your life as part of God's plan for all of creation can be found and followed. We, you, have a limited time on this earth and after that … eternity. I encourage you to find your way to Jesus.

If the following prayer will help you get started on your journey to Him, please read it from your heart. As you come to Him, He will come to you.

Father, I want You in my life. Please forgive my past and lead me to the future. I believe that You have a plan for my life, and I want to follow You. Thank you, Father. In Jesus' name. Amen

ABOUT THE AUTHOR

R. Hilary Adcock is an architect, a general aviation pilot, and a Christian. His firm consults on projects in Arizona, California, Colorado, New Mexico, and Nevada. His personal relationship with Jesus has survived life's failures and victories since his salvation in 1969. He currently lives in San Diego with his wife and children.